INTO THE MISTS

LAURA GREENWOOD

SKYE MACKINNON

Peryton Press

CONTENTS

Before you start   vii
What Happened Before   xi
The Seven Wardens Series   xiii
The Seven Wardens   xv

Chapter 1   1
Illustration: Luch   15
Chapter 2   17
Illustration: Beithir   37
Chapter 3   39
Illustration: Ceasg   63
Chapter 4   65
Chapter 5   81
Chapter 6   105
Illustration: Aos Sìth   115
Chapter 7   117
Illustration: Seelie   129
Chapter 8   131
Chapter 9   143
Chapter 10   149
Chapter 11   159
Chapter 12   169
Illustration: Sheet Music   185
Chapter 13   187
Illustration: St. Kilda   207
Chapter 14   209
Chapter 15   219
Illustration: Selkie   231
Chapter 16   233

Chapter 17   245
Epilogue   259

Glossary   271
About Skye MacKinnon   273
About Laura Greenwood   275

BEFORE YOU START

This book is also available as audiobook!

The Seven Wardens series is a reverse harem, one woman and multiple love interests. Macey does not have to choose.

Please note that the authors of this book are from the UK, and as such, spellings and some turns of phrase will appear in British English.

You can find a glossary at the end of this book.

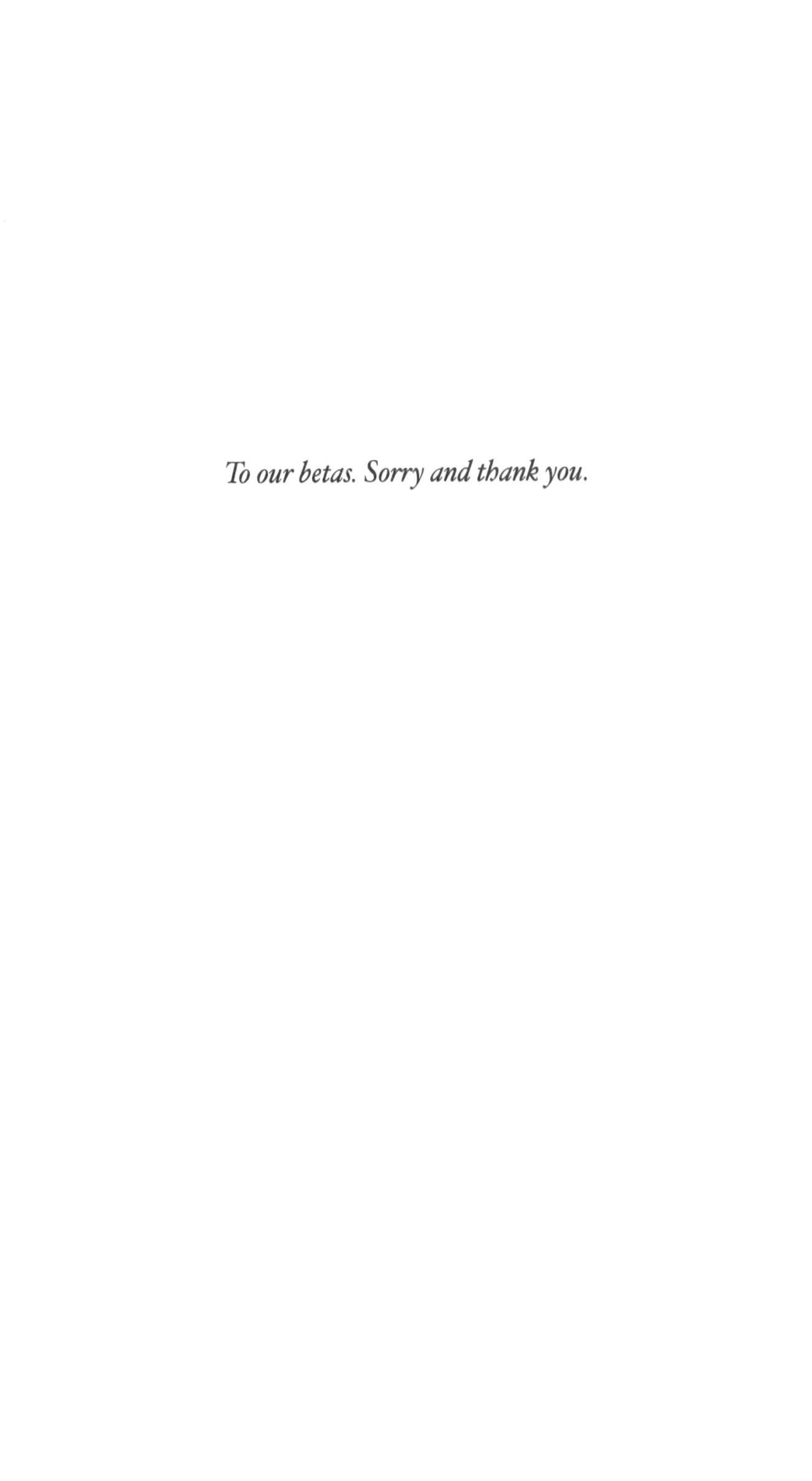

To our betas. Sorry and thank you.

Once upon a time, there was a kelpie princess who was kidnapped by her Princes Charming - yes, there were three of them. Two wraiths and one incubus, and all three of them made her hormones dance. They even did a bit of kissing and fondling.

Sadly, there was a problem with the Staran, the mythical pathways enabling them to travel. So, they sat out to find an answer and came upon blue, scary-looking people living beneath the sea, a cat shifter and his dog shifter sister (she died, oops), a blue-haired mage named Izban, and a mysterious Voice that gave Macey a lot of pain and distress.

In the end, that evil being kidnapped our little kelpie, which is why we're now giving you the second book to read. Enjoy!

1. From the Deeps (Audiobook Available)
2. Into the Mists (Audiobook Available)
3. Beneath the Earth
4. Within the Flames
5. Above the Waves
6. Under the Ice
7. Rule the Dark

- Through the Storms (optional spin-off between books 1 & 2)
- Below the Baubles (optional short story between books 5 & 6)
- Beyond the Loch (optional novella set before the events of the Seven Wardens series)
- Inside the Egg (novella set after the events of the Seven Wardens series)

- Seven Wardens Boxed Set: Books 1-4
- Seven Wardens Boxed Set: Books 5-7
- Seven Wardens: The Complete Series

THE SEVEN WARDENS

Water: Macey (Kelpie)
Wind: Cam (Wraith)
Fire: Flint (Wraith)
Earth: Jared (Incubus)
Ice: Izban (Mage)
Lightning: Amber (Beithir)
Air: ?

Akelpie, an incubus and two wraiths walked into a bar. A human mage trailed behind them, a slightly bored expression on his face. They were here to see the Loch Ness monster, also lovingly known as Aunt Nessie.

It was a pub as Scottish as they came. Slightly dark, slightly smelly, and full of loud people. A sign by the door announced live music later that evening and Macey was a little sad that they'd likely be gone by then.

This was Aunt Nessie's favourite haunt. She knew most of the local fishermen and had helped a few of the tourist businesses in the village to see a glimpse of 'the monster'. Not that she was actually a monster. She was a kelpie, just like Macey, but her temperament was a little more volatile. She was a loud and very determined old lady who didn't take no for an answer. Macey loved her aunt and had always found her advice invaluable. Which was why she was taking the others to see her.

She spotted Nessie in a corner, surrounded by a few older men, all of them wearing the thick oilskins the fishermen here preferred. They certainly weren't in here for a pint, judging from the agitated manner they were talking to her. In contrast, Nessie was looking relaxed, calmly sipping on her large glass of the local frothy ale.

However, she did look a little relieved when she spotted Macey making her way through the crowd.

"My baby niece, come over here!"

"Baby niece?" Cam chuckled and Macey elbowed him in the ribs.

"Not a word. My brothers are older so I've always been her youngest niece."

"Don't think we won't forget this," Jared laughed. "My little baby."

She aimed at him with her other elbow but hit Izban instead.

"Watch it!"

"Sorry," she muttered. Izban and her were still not on the best terms. They were both headstrong, and neither liked agreeing with the other's opinions. Even if they were right, in Macey's case. Her three men seemed to be okay with having the mage around, but she was going to need some more time to get used to it. If he wasn't one of the Seven Wardens, she'd tell him to fuck off.

"Feasgar mhath," Macey greeted her aunt in Gaelic. "Everything okay with these gentlemen?" She shot them a curious look. Everybody loved Nessie, so seeing them argue with her was very strange.

"These 'gentlemen'," the older kelpie emphasised the last word, "were just about to leave me the hell alone before I tell their wives what they've been up to."

That got the men muttering amongst themselves, before one of them said angrily, "We'll be back tomorrow, and the day after, until you tell us." He left and the others followed them, leaving some empty seats for Macey and her guys to take.

She gave her aunt a quick hug and sat down on the wooden bench next to her. "Good to see you, auntie."

"And you. I didn't expect you, is something wrong?"

"There's a lot going on that I can't go into right now," Macey said, trying not to give too much away. Aunt Nessie may be formidable but she was also getting old and she didn't want to worry her. "But I need some advice."

Nessie chuckled. "Oh no, not like that, young

lady. I want the full story, gossip and all. Make it a juicy tale, then you can have my advice."

Macey launched into the twisty tale that has somehow landed her here. Even as she spoke, she realised how ridiculous it all sounded; to her own ears as well as to anyone else's. Who was going to believe the things she'd seen and done? That she'd been under a dome in the sea? Or in a house in the mists? Not to mention being hunted by a disembodied voice that just appeared in her head at the worst possible point in time.

But, to her relief, Aunt Nessie not only listened, but she nodded along, clearly understanding the complexity of the journey Macey and her Wardens had been on. She didn't even interrupt to ask to be introduced to Macey's men, which was actually a little out of character. Aunt Nessie was no shrinking violet, if she wanted to know something, then she'd butt in the moment she thought of it and demand to know it.

Macey stumbled in her retelling, and a wide grin spread over Aunt Nessie's face. That was never a good sign. Normally it meant mischief, but there was something sinister about the look she was currently giving her niece.

Something wasn't right here. But Macey couldn't put her finger on what. And why was she here and not in the warehouse with the men? Her last memory had been of meeting Izban, and trying to convince the mage that he should travel with them. He'd agreed so long as they went to save Amber, who oddly wasn't here with them.

It definitely wasn't right. She knew her guys, no way would they be this cool and collected if they knew someone needed saving.

"What's going on here?" she asked, her voice shaking. Aunt Nessie's smile broadened, filling her with dread. No, something definitely wasn't right here.

"What do you think is going on?" Aunt Nessie's question set off all kinds of red flags in Macey's mind. It wasn't something the older woman would ask. She'd tease and prod for Macey to work it out herself, but she wouldn't be quite so sinister about it...

"Auntie?"

"You don't seem certain."

Beside Macey, her men stayed suspiciously quiet. She knew they'd leave her to do the talking if they thought that was what she wanted, but at least one of them should have offered her some support right now, even if it was just a gentle touch. She liked it when they did that, it gave her a satisfied sense of support. Made her feel loved and wanted in a way no one else had ever quite managed.

"This isn't real," she murmured to herself, not quite believing it. She'd been in a lot of outlandish situations recently, this could just have been one of those, but she doubted it. "This isn't real," she repeated, louder this time, and she made sure to look into Aunt Nessie's eyes.

The twin orbs swirled with darkness, completely unlike the moss green eyes her aunt usually had. Macey was right. She had to be. This *wasn't* her aunt. And though it was possible, she doubted this was actually happening.

A chilling laugh filled the air and her heart sank. There was only one person that was going to be...

WORKED IT OUT, LITTLE KELPIE?

Macey shuddered, and the world went black.

SHE JOLTED UPRIGHT, taking in the dark cell around her. She was relieved the weird dream was over, not quite so much over her surroundings. After a few blinks, memories came rushing back in, and it all slotted into place.

She was a prisoner.

This was her cell.

The Voice had her.

"This is hopeless." Her voice came out as a whine and she instantly hated herself for it. She wasn't the kind of woman who'd just take what she was given. She could sort this out. She wasn't sure how, but damned if she was going to wait around to be saved. Her Wardens would have a field day if she did that.

"I'd hardly say hopeless." The small squeaky voice broke through her inner misery, and made Macey jump. She glanced around the room a few times, trying to find where it'd come from. This voice hadn't sounded hostile, but what did she know? Nothing was as it seemed, according to her recent experiences.

"Where are you?" she asked quietly.

"On the windowsill," the voice replied instantly. Looking in the direction of the tiny window, that definitely wasn't big enough to warrant the name, Macey gave her own squeak of surprise.

"You're a mouse." It was smaller than one of her hands, with dark brown fur and intelligent eyes.

"Thank you, Captain Obvious," the mouse replied. "Though I much prefer Luch."

"Is that your name?"

"Of a sorts. It's what you can call me." It scratched behind one of its ears with a paw, studying her intently.

"Why am I talking to a mouse?" she asked herself quietly.

"Better than talking to yourself."

And why was the mouse such a smart ass? She was

hundreds of times bigger than he was, even with her tiny stature.

"It just seems unlikely."

"Says the walking, talking, water horse," it replied.

Macey growled low in her throat. "Don't call me a water horse."

"Don't call me a mouse then. I told you, I prefer Luch." It seemed pretty serious, and she didn't want to annoy the only thing she could talk to in this place.

"Okay, I'm sorry, Luch. I'm just grumpy from being imprisoned and all."

The mouse, no, Luch, chuckled. "You're not the only one. Though I think the other woman is nearly mad. She rocks a lot." Luch frowned.

"Other woman?" Macey perked up. While being imprisoned herself wasn't exactly a good sign, if the other woman was Amber, then she might be able to turn this around. Being in the same place as the person she was trying to rescue was a good start. Even if she technically needed rescuing herself.

"Yes, red hair, very skinny. Too much so for my tastes."

Macey ignored the last comment. Not quite wanting to think about what kind of tastes a mouse could possibly have. But Amber didn't sound to be in good shape. And in the Voice's tender care, that wasn't a good sign. She tried to work out how long the Lightning Warden had been here, but she didn't recall Izban or Sharrara mentioning a specific time frame.

One thing was for certain though, Macey needed to get out of here quickly. She needed to find the other woman and get her out too. And try not to go too crazy. If talking to Luch didn't already make that too late.

"There's two men too. Whiny ones. I got bored of them, so I'm glad you're here now."

"So where are we, exactly?"

The mouse shrugged and Macey tried not to laugh despite the seriousness of the situation. Watching a mouse shrug was one of the most hilarious things she'd ever seen.

"I was born here, never left the place. You're in the dungeon, and there's about twenty floors above you. It's a big castle, from what others say." He shrugged again. "I've never seen another one, so couldn't tell you if that's true."

"Twenty floors? Yes, that's definitely big. Now, can you help me get out of here?"

"Nah, I don't get involved. It's not worth the trouble."

Macey sighed. Of course, it couldn't have been as easy as that. Otherwise Amber wouldn't still be here.

"Come on, don't you want to see the world? You could come with me."

Luch shook his little furry head and jumped down

from the window sill, somehow managing not to hurt himself. "You're not the first to try and you won't be the last. I like my tail intact, so don't ask me again."

He ran over the uneven stone floor and jumped through the bars at the other end of the cell.

"Wait!" Macey called, but it was too late, the mouse had gone.

TIME PASSED VERY SLOWLY. She knew the Voice would return. She knew she'd only be alone and undisturbed in this cell for so long. Of course, she'd tried opening the door to her cell, but even with her kelpie strength it didn't budge. And of course, she'd tried to use magic, but it was as if she was trying to grasp air, her magic just wouldn't listen to her commands. It was different from having it locked up inside her. She could still feel it, but she couldn't get a hold on it. No wonder Amber hadn't escaped yet. She'd been wondering about that. From the few things Izban had told them about Lightning, she was strong.

Macey paced from wall to wall, counting her steps. The cell wasn't very large, six steps in each direction. The tiny window was the only source of light, and it was beginning to get dark outside. She'd tried to look out of the window, but it was too high up. There was no furniture she could have used to stand on, all she had was a filthy blanket she'd avoided even touching. It was a stereotypical dungeon, except that she didn't even get a bucket to do her business in. There was a small hole in the floor in one of the corners and Macey dreaded having to pee through there. Nobody had given her any water or food so far, so at least she could deal with that problem later.

Although her stomach was starting to make itself noticeable. Somehow, she didn't think she'd get proper food here, but right now, she'd be grateful even for some bread.

She sat down in the middle of the room which seemed to be the cleanest bit of the floor. It was getting cold in the cell, but the blanket wasn't tempting her yet. She could almost see the fleas living in it.

It was strangely silent. No shouts, no talking, not even footsteps. Knowing the Voice, she had expected tortured screams, but of course she was glad she didn't have to hear those. From what Luch had said, there were at least three other prisoners, Amber and two men. Were the men connected to the Wardens somehow? Was one of them Air, perhaps? But according to the prophecy, Air was the last of the Wardens to join them, and who knew if it even was a male. It could be another woman.

How long had she been here now? Macey wasn't sure. It could have been hours or days; after her dream experience earlier, she knew she couldn't assume anything in this place. Maybe this cell wasn't even real. Maybe she was still with her men, locked inside her mind, the Voice making her think that she was imprisoned. Everything was possible, and that scared her. She'd always been able to rely on her senses and her mind, but right now, she couldn't trust herself.

There was a noise in the distance and she jumped to her feet. Better be ready.

Footsteps were coming closer, but they stopped before they reached her cell. The sound of a door opening gave her hope. Was someone letting them out? Were her fellow Wardens here to rescue them?

"Get up," a rasping voice said in the distance and her hopes evaporated into nothing. That didn't sound like someone friendly.

"Get up, I said!"

The sound of a slap on bare skin made Macey shiver. So, it wasn't just mental violence the prisoners here had to endure. Now she was hoping the man wouldn't come to her cell. She'd rather go hungry than be beaten.

Something - perhaps someone - was dragged along the corridor, away from Macey. She didn't hear the cell door close, so she assumed whoever had been in there was now with the man. Soon, silence fell again. The last light outside disappeared and Macey was left in darkness, cowering in the middle of the cell, trying not to think of what was happening to the other prisoner.

Luch

2

Waiting was torture. Macey laughed at the thought. Could she really say that ever again, given what she'd been hearing during her stay here? It'd been a couple of days at the most, probably not even that, and yet she was sure she'd be affected by this for the rest of her life.

When her Wardens had kidnapped her, she'd been annoyed at first. But ultimately, they'd treated her with nothing but respect and kindness. More than that when they were...

No. Those thoughts weren't for here. She wasn't going to sully the memories by thinking about them in this godforsaken place.

"Put off, put off, and row with speed,
For now's the time, and the hour of need!"

Macey sang to herself softly, her voice shaking

with the strain. Remembering one of the old songs her mother used to sing to her was helping to drown out the screams and the pleas. She was suddenly very glad of her mother's love of folk songs.

"One of the men was singing that," a familiar voice said, and she looked up to find Luch perched on the windowsill. She shouldn't be surprised, he only really disappeared when she tried to press him further on things.

"Sorry?" She wasn't quite sure what he meant.

"The song you were singing, *Queen Mary's Escape from Loch Leven,* if I'm not mistaken." He sounded very sure of himself, especially for a mouse.

"What about it?" she asked, nodding her head.

"One of the male prisoners. He was singing it. Well, humming more accurately. According to the other man, he shouldn't even try the singing."

Macey perked up. That sounded a lot like how Bruce and Jerry would act. Bruce loved to sing under his breath but couldn't to save his life. And if the song he'd been humming had been *Queen Mary*, then it seemed likely that the men in question were her brothers. And if they were...

"What do they look like?" she asked eagerly, hope welling up within her for the first time. She wasn't sure why. There was probably just as little she could do with her brothers down the hall, as she could by herself, but it was something to strive for. And hopefully, if it was them, she could get to the bottom of how they were involved in it all too.

She really shouldn't get her hopes up.

"Men," the mouse said, running its paw over its ear and scratching.

"Not what I meant. Do they look like me?" she asked, heart pounding in her chest as she waited for the answer.

"They're the same shape without the..." The mouse made a gesture around its chest, clearly intending to mean boobs. Despite herself, Macey laughed before firmly clamping her hand over her mouth. She didn't want the guards to hear her, or they'd likely come to investigate. Something that wasn't likely to end all that well for her and would certainly mean that Luch disappeared off to wherever he hid when he wasn't with her.

"No, I mean hair, eyes, voice..." she trailed off, now worrying she'd completely got the wrong end of the stick. It'd wouldn't be good for her mentally if she thought she could save her brothers only for them to turn out to be complete strangers.

That was uncharitable. Saving strangers wouldn't be a bad thing. Quite the contrary. But it also wouldn't be the same as saving her brothers.

"I suppose so, yes. But they're a little bit...bigger than you."

"Taller?" she asked eagerly. "Wider? Stronger? Are

they kelpies too?" Why hadn't she thought to ask that sooner? Luch had known what she was, so it was to be expected that he knew what others were imprisoned here too. Her mind strayed to Amber again. She wondered what she was. It seemed unlikely she was just another mage, not from the way Izban was talking about her. But Macey couldn't think of any creature connected to lightning. Maybe her education was lacking in that respect. It wasn't like it affected her people at the bottom of their Loch.

"Yes, yes, not anymore, and I think so. But their aura is a bit funny." Luch scrunched up his nose in a rather comical gesture.

"Funny how?"

Seconds seemed to drag as Macey waited for him to answer. But just when he was about to answer, the loud sound of boots thudding against a hard floor filled the room, and she froze in position. Luch did the same on the windowsill, while exchanging worried looks with her.

"Go," Macey mouthed to him, and he nodded, waving goodbye with one paw and turning to disappear into the wall. Macey cocked her head to the side. Her life really had taken a turn towards the weird recently.

She waited with baited breath as the boots approached, and something deep within her gut told her that this time she wasn't escaping. This time, it was her turn.

Macey's blood turned to ice, and panic began to build within her. Even if there wasn't anything she could do, her fight or flight instinct kicked in. She wasn't naive enough to believe she was stronger than the guards. The Voice really wouldn't leave security in his prison to off chance. They'd outnumber her, and they'd probably be more powerful than her. Their magic likely wouldn't be blocked either.

That just pissed her off. How *dare* the Voice kidnap her. Her men would be worried sick. And hopefully on their way. It'd save her so much time if they were already here and she didn't have to find them when she escaped.

Plus, she'd need Flint and Cam to get her brothers back to the Loch. No matter how to blame they were or weren't, she wanted them out of the way.

A scratching sound in the door confirmed Macey's fear. It really *was* her turn. Despite every instinct telling her to turn around, she refused. If this was going to be her last day, then she was going to give at least one last act of defiance.

She wouldn't scream either. No matter what they did to her. Okay, that one was a lie. There'd no doubt come a point where she'd have to scream, but until then, not even a whimper would cross her lips.

"Time to go, Princess," a male voice sneered. It

was the same guard she'd heard before, and dread joined the panic.

Instead of letting him drag her, she turned around and looked him in the eye. "Okay, lead the way."

"Oh no, that's not how we do things here. Stretch out your hands."

She only hesitated for a moment, but it was enough for the guard to backhand her. Her cheek was burning and she instinctively covered it with one hand - which the guard used to grab her by the wrist and put a bronze cuff around it.

A shiver went through Macey. Bronze. Oh no. People thought iron was painful to supernaturals, but that was a rumour the fae had spread to protect themselves. In fact, it was bronze they were allergic to. The fae more than most other supernatural species, but for kelpies, it was almost as bad. It didn't hurt physically, but it blocked their magic and their ability to shift. The Voice really had to know a lot about kelpies to use bronze cuffs on her.

Momentarily distracted by the empty feeling spreading through her chest, the guard took her other hand and clipped on the other cuff. He attached a thick rope to the shackles and without another word, started to walk out of the cell, dragging Macey behind him.

She was weak from days without food and struggled to catch up. The fear of being dragged across the dirty ground was all that kept her going.

They passed rows of cells. It was too dark to see if there were any prisoners in there, but if there were, they stayed quiet.

Just when Macey thought that she wouldn't be able to walk for much longer without collapsing, they reached a staircase. Without warning, the guard grabbed her around the waist and threw her over his shoulder as if she was a sack of potatoes.

"Oi!" Macey shouted but it came out as a whimper. She'd not had water since yesterday and her voice was suffering.

In response, the man hit her hard on her bum. She whimpered again both in pain and humiliation. So far, none of the guards had touched her, but it looked like this particular one might be different. And right now, she was completely at his mercy. With her hands shackled, her magic blocked and not able to shift, there wasn't much she could do to defend herself should he start to grope her.

He didn't put her back on the ground when they reached the end of the staircase, but instead continued to carry her on his shoulder. His bones were pressing into her abdomen and it was getting harder for her to breathe. She was almost hoping that they'd reach their destination soon, even though she knew it would probably be worse than what she was going through right now.

They - well, the guard - walked along a bleak corridor before turning right into a courtyard. Macey was expecting to see daylight, but instead, white mist surrounded them. It seemed even thicker than what she was used to from the Staran and it smelled strange... like something was rotting close by. Decay. She started breathing through her mouth, but even so she could taste the wrongness of the mist.

The guard dropped her unceremoniously in the centre of the courtyard and bound the rope connected to her shackles to a pole next to them. She felt as if she was a dog being left behind while its owner did their shopping, and tears of humiliation burned in her eyes.

How the waves did she end up here? And how could she escape?

THERE IS NO ESCAPE, LITTLE KELPIE.

The Voice was booming in her head, louder than ever. She instinctively wanted to cover her ears, but her hands were cuffed.

"What do you want?" she asked feebly, realising how pathetic that sounded.

OH, NOTHING IMPORTANT. ALL I NEED IS YOUR SOUL.

He laughed and Macey thought her head would explode. It hurt so much. Stars were dancing in front of her eyes and her ears were pounding. She was almost hoping that she'd faint from the pain. At least then she wouldn't have to be conscious during whatever he was going to do with her.

NO, YOU WILL STAY AWAKE. YOU WILL FEEL PAIN, YOU WILL FEEL FEAR. I NEED YOU TO SUFFER OR YOU WON'T BE ANY USE TO ME.

"Why? How is that going to help you hurt the Staran?"

She was feeling a bit like she was in a film by now. Keep the bad guy talking in the hope that he'll reveal his evil plans. Even if that meant taking those secrets to the grave.

IS THAT WHAT YOU THINK? THAT I WANT TO DESTROY THE STARAN? OH LITTLE KELPIE, YOU HAVE NO IDEA HOW WRONG YOU ARE.

"Then why else are you doing this? Why do you need the Wardens?"

I DON'T NEED YOU. I JUST DON'T WANT YOU TO FULFILL YOUR PURPOSE. SO NOW THAT I HAVE YOU HERE, YOU'RE LIKE ANY OTHER OF MY PRISONERS. I'M GOING TO ENJOY PLAYING WITH YOU THOUGH, YOU HAVE SPIRIT. AND IF YOU'RE STILL AS BRAVE IN THE END, I WILL EAT YOUR SOUL WITH DELIGHT.

"Eat my soul? How is that even possible?"

YOU WILL SEE. SOON. NOW, LET'S HAVE SOME FUN.

There were sounds in the distance. A woman shouting something. Through the thick mist, two people approached. One was the same guard who had brought Macey here, and the other... a young woman around Macey's age, maybe a bit younger. She looked almost too thin to stand and her eyes had a crazed look, even from a distance. She had a bronze collar around her neck, but she wasn't being dragged by the guard. No, she was walking passively by his side.

Macey had a sinking feeling about who the girl might be. And she didn't like that thought one bit.

TWO WARDENS UNDER MY CONTROL. YOU STAND NO CHANCE NOW, LITTLE KELPIE.

The other girl's head whipped up, and her eyes widened, panic filling them.

"You," she blurted, half seeming afraid, half relieved. It was almost like she knew who Macey was. Which was impossible, surely?

"Me?"

One of the guards kicked her in the shin, and she hissed, but didn't cry out. She had bigger things to worry about. Like what would happen if the Voice decided to make Amber attack her. For she had no doubt this *was* the woman she needed to find.

Lightning and water didn't really mix. It almost sounded kind of deadly, and Macey wasn't completely keen on finding out how so.

"You've finally come to kill me then?" Amber met Macey's eyes with a strange mix of resignation and determination in her gaze. As broken as she looked on the inside, this girl was still standing, and still fighting. Just not in the most obvious of ways.

"Why would I want to kill you?" Macey frowned, genuinely confused about what she could mean. She'd never really wanted to kill anyone. Not until the Voice anyway. She'd quite happily carve his heart out with a rusty spoon if she got the chance. If he had one. A heart that was. She was sure finding a rusty spoon would be reasonably straight-forward.

"My dre-"

ENOUGH!

Amber flinched alongside Macey. Interesting. The Voice was talking to them both then. That was particularly interesting given their stays here.

The echo of his words faded away, but Amber continued to flinch. He must still be talking to her then. Poor girl.

"No... don't make me... no... please... no." She started clawing at her face, as if to get the Voice out. Macey wondered if that was what she looked like when the Voice was in her head. If so, it made sense why her men were always so worried after she'd come around.

A pang of loss shot through her heart. She wanted them with her so badly. Not because she'd need them to escape, but just because they made her feel more complete.

ENJOY, LITTLE KELPIE, the Voice taunted.

Macey braced herself as best she could, wishing her wrists weren't still shackled. She wasn't quite sure what the Voice had in mind, but given everything she'd heard and witnessed so far, likelihood was that it wasn't going to be pleasant.

She wouldn't scream though. She had to keep that promise. Giving him the satisfaction would be the worst possible torture.

"No, no, no, no, no." Amber glanced down at her hands with an expression of horror on her face.

Macey looked down too and gulped. The girl's hands were covered in sparks of electricity. She guessed she really was about to find out what happened when electricity and water mixed. She was scared. Actually, no. That was an understatement. She was petrified. But still determined not to let the Voice see that. He'd be far too satisfied, and she'd love to wipe the smug expression out of his tone.

"I'm sorry," Amber whispered, meeting Macey's eyes again.

"I know," Macey replied, trying to tell her it was

alright. And failing badly. They were just two young women in the courtyard of an unknown place, and in the grasp of a sadistic... something. How did she still not know what the Voice was? How was she going to defeat a mystery?

The electricity began to build, and storm clouds rolled overhead. What the hell was Amber? Or was it even her causing this?

"Please forgive me," the redhead begged.

"Always," Macey responded, before lightning crashed down from the sky, landing just feet away from where she stood. Despite herself, Macey flinched away.

"No," Amber tried again, tears beginning to stream down her face, and her mouth set into a determined line.

If Macey had to guess, she'd have said that the Voice had the other woman in her grip, and the fact the lightning had missed her at all, was simply testament to Amber's sense of control. Most likely due to being locked up for so long.

Macey had to admire that. If they both got out of here alive, then she was going to have to ask. Maybe. Or maybe not. She was already looking forward to forgetting her own time here after all.

In front of her, Amber dropped to her knees, screaming in anguish. This was it then, the moment she lost control. Macey closed her eyes, thinking that not seeing it coming would make the pain easier to bear.

It didn't. The waiting was almost worse than the pain.

The crackle of lightning coming had her on edge, and she could almost feel it approaching. Thinking of Flint, Jared and Cam as hard as she could, Macey managed to distract herself.

But only for a moment.

The electricity hit her skin, and a singed hair smell surrounded her. But oddly, not as much pain as she expected. Hardly any at all in fact. It was as if the lightning was one with her, though she couldn't quite wield it.

She opened her eyes, meeting Amber's surprised face, before smiling slightly. The other girl picked up on what was happening quickly, or she had if the echoing smile was anything to go by. Even so, she stayed on her knees. Hopefully the Voice either couldn't tell what was happening or couldn't do anything about it.

Macey felt another surge of electricity as the lightning strike grew stronger. She was even more impressed with Amber now. Even though the Voice had managed to make her use her powers, she'd still managed to hold some back. That must take a lot of mental fortitude.

Twin prickles around her wrists, followed by two

loud cracks, had Macey smiling maniacally. The copper restraints were gone, fallen to the floor in pieces, and allowing a surge of her own magic to join Amber's.

NO!

The Voice seemed to have figured out what was happening. Too bad it was too little, too late. Macey directed their combined powers around them, knocking the Voice's men to the ground with the combined lethality of water and electricity.

They probably didn't survive, but she also didn't really care. She'd heard and seen enough, both in person, and from what Luch had said.

It wasn't until the surge of magic began to fade, that she noticed the slight stinging sensation on her lower back. This time, she didn't wonder what it was about. It was more painful than the marks she'd received from sex, but she was hardly complaining. Izban hadn't seemed like the sharing type anyway.

Her clothes were wet and the courtyard ground had turned into one giant puddle. She hadn't even noticed she'd summoned that much water.

Now what? Her shackles had gone and she was free to run, but where to? There were two doors leading away from the courtyard: one was the door her jailor had brought her, the other straight opposite. It looked more inviting. Wherever it led, at least it wasn't to the dungeons.

Macey began to run towards the door, expecting Amber to follow - but when she reached it, there was no sign of the redhead behind her. She looked back and saw Amber standing still in the same spot, tiny bolts of lightning flashing around her wrists. She was wavering, reaching for something in front of her that wasn't there.

Then she collapsed.

Macey ran back, cursing herself for not checking on Amber first. The girl had been in captivity for far longer than herself; of course she wasn't well. The exhaustion of using so much magic at once must have been too much for her frail body.

Luckily, Amber hadn't passed out completely. She was lying on her side, her eyes open, but obviously too weak to stand.

"I'm sorry," she whispered faintly, but Macey shushed her.

"Do you know the way out of here?"

"I think so." Amber groaned. "But it's hard to know what was real and what wasn't."

"It's better than randomly running around this place. Imagine running as fast as you can, how long would it take?"

"The main gate isn't far from here. Maybe two minutes? But I can't walk, let alone run."

Macey ignored that last statement. "Do you think you'll be able to hold onto me?"

Amber frowned in confusion. "You don't look strong enough to carry me. Better leave me here and get out while you still can. I'm sure the Voice will be back soon."

Macey chuckled. "Believe me, I'm strong enough. But don't tell anyone. And be quick, I can only hold my breath for so long."

Amber looked even more confused now, but Macey didn't have time to explain. Instead, she showed her. She shifted.

Shifting outside of the loch was hard, but there was enough water on her clothes and the ground for her to manage. It was painful, though, but she couldn't think of any other way of getting Amber out of here.

When she had fully shifted into her kelpie form, she knelt down beside Amber, nudging the girl to climb onto her back. This was the first time anyone who wasn't a kelpie was going to ride on her. It was a shameful thing to do; kelpies were incredibly proud creatures. But this was an emergency and if she was lucky, nobody in her family would ever find out.

That's when she remembered her brothers. If the two men in the dungeons even were her brothers, but it was too much of a coincidence.

She huffed. Get Amber out first, that was the priority. Then go back and get her brothers. Somehow. A problem for a later time. Right now, her problem was that she was having to hold her breath and already felt a slight sting in her lungs. Kelpies weren't made to be out of water for long. That's why the legends of kelpies pulling humans underwater to eat them were bollocks. Kelpies couldn't keep their heads out of water for long enough to first find and then attack a human. Besides that, they were vegetarians.

Amber climbed onto Macey's broad back and clung to her mane. As gentle as she could, the kelpie got to her feet and began to move towards the door. When she was sure Amber had a good grip on her, she broke into a run, following the girl's whispered directions.

From the courtyard they entered a long, dim corridor that led into another, even dimmer one. On and on they ran, around corners, through doors. There were no people to be seen anywhere. Macey found that very strange, but she didn't have time to ponder on that, nor on the fact that the Voice wasn't talking to them anymore or trying to keep them in his grasp.

No, she was focused on not breathing.

Her kelpie lungs were better than her human ones, but by now she was quickly running out of oxygen. Finally, they exited the building they were in and entered another drawn out courtyard. At the end was a gate.

It was closed.

Nonetheless, Macey continued to gallop towards it. Freedom was so close.

Suddenly, two guards stepped out of a small door beside the gate. They held out their hands, intent on stopping the girls escape.

Mages.

Oh waves, what was she going to do?

"I can break down the gate, but I'll pass out after that," Amber whispered.

That meant the guards were Macey's responsibility. She whinnied in response to show her rider she agreed with her plan.

Her lungs were burning, she knew she had less than a minute left before she'd have to shift back. Summoning her water magic, she threw two balls of water at the guards without warning. One of them deflected his, but the other was hit hard and slammed against the wall behind him. He sank to the ground, unconscious.

Only one to go. Macey readied another water ball, but the guard was now on the offensive. He threw a fire lance at her and she just about managed to jump to the side to evade it. However, it gave her the opening to thrust her own watery missile and hit the mage before he could create another lance. Just like his fellow guard, he slumped to the ground.

Lightning tore from the sky and into the metal

gate. Electricity fizzled through the air and the gate's doors sprung open.

Using the last of her energy, Macey ran through the open gate and along the drawbridge that was leading away from the castle.

Beithir

3

"Do you really think prodding her is a good idea?" a male voice asked.

Macey wondered what that was even about until a sharp prod came at her shoulder. She groaned. No, prodding her was not a good idea. And if she could just summon the strength, the person on the other end of that finger would regret it.

"Do you have any better ideas?" the prodder responded.

"No. But go tend to your own girlfriend."

The people around her, and she was sure there were a few, lapsed into silence.

"She's not my girlfriend," the prodder protested.

"Besides, I'm fine," a weak Amber replied.

Wait...if Amber was the girlfriend, then that must

have meant the prodder was Izban. And if Izban was here...

Macey's head began to clear, and she shakily pushed her arms underneath her. She turned as she rose and was greeted by three worried sets of eyes. And Izban's, but he just looked more exasperated than anything else.

"You're okay!" Flint fell to his knees and pulled her into his arms, peppering her face with kisses. "We were so worried."

"Alright, let the rest of us in," Jared grumbled, but it was impossible to miss the relief in his tone.

Flint let her go, and Macey slowly got herself to her feet. She could sense all three of them fretting already, but appreciated that they were leaving her to it. At least they knew her well enough to realise interfering wasn't in their best interests.

The moment she was steady again, she found herself pulled into a bear hug from Jared, and on the receiving end of the doting smile from Cam.

"I knew you could do it," he said softly. She smiled at him. While she was glad they were here, she was also more than a little smug that she was the one who'd saved herself. And Amber for that matter.

"Thanks," she said, twisting out of Jared's arms, and going up on her toes to kiss him. He responded in kind, keeping the pressure light, and the attention on her in a far more loving way than her men usually showed. Normally they were in the more taking-her frame of mind. They must have been really scared for her safety...

Warmth flowed through Macey at the thought, and her heart swelled to three times its normal size. Though maybe that was just the lack of oxygen. That could do funny things to kelpies.

"Here," Amber said, handing her a bottle of water. "You must be running low."

"Thanks." Macey unscrewed the cap after taking it, and chugged down the water, surprised by just how much she actually needed it. She was a water being, she shouldn't have let herself get so low. "How did you find us?" she asked her men after the bottle was empty.

"We didn't," Flint replied, shuffling his feet slightly, as if uncomfortable.

"You can't tell me you're here just by chance," she said.

"Of course not," Cam butted in. "But it was actually Izban casting a searching spell for Amber that led us here."

Macey exchanged glances with the red-headed girl, who shrugged.

"Must be possible."

"You don't know what he's capable of?" Macey replied, raising an eyebrow.

"We only met a little before I was kidnapped,"

Amber said, a blush staining her cheeks as she tried not to look at the Ice Warden. Interesting.

Macey counted herself lucky that she already had the Lightning mark on her back. Hopefully, she'd be able to add the Ice mark in a similar fashion. That way she wouldn't have to get between what was clearly a blossoming relationship.

It was also a small relief. Three men was proving difficult enough at the moment, particularly with their protective streaks. She didn't want to add another man *and* woman into the equation. She wouldn't even have known where to start if she'd needed to have a relationship with Amber.

"Alright then. Next steps," Macey announced, ignoring the fact she was naked from bursting through her clothes while shifted.

Cam shrugged off his jacket and handed it to her, and she took it gratefully, wrapping it around herself and enjoying his scent as it wafted to her nose.

"We need to get out of here and make a plan," Jared said.

"No," three voices responded all at once. Macey frowned. She knew why she was saying no to him. But why were Amber and Izban?

"Who wants to go first?" Flint asked, amusement dancing in his eyes.

"I think my brothers are in there," Macey said.

"I'm not having Amber in danger again," Izban spoke over the top of her, glaring at her men.

"Now hang on a minute," Amber said, putting her hands on her hips. "You're not the boss of me, Izban. I'm not sitting back and letting the Voice get away with this."

Despite having been in captivity for who knows how long, the other woman looked surprisingly strong, and Macey wouldn't mess with her if she didn't have to.

"You've been in there for weeks, Amber, no one can expect you to go back there," Izban countered, his voice softening with unspent emotions.

"That hardly matters. Do you think the bastard is going to wait for me to recover his strength? Besides, you let me fly during that storm. You can't complain that this is any more or less dangerous." She crossed her arms and fixed him with a look.

But all Macey wanted to know about was her use of the word fly. What *was* the red-head? Up until that moment, Macey had just assumed she was some kind of storm mage, but it sounded like that wasn't the case.

"That was before you were kidnapped. You look half-starved, Amber..."

The other woman couldn't have looked angrier if she'd tried, and Macey took a moment to fix her men with a knowing look. They knew if they ever tried to do this to her, then they might as well wish they were dead.

"So why did you two want to go back into the castle?" Flint interceded, earning himself an angry look from both Izban and Amber.

"I didn't want to go there," Izban protested. "I just meant that we didn't want to come with you four. This is where Amber and I go our own way."

Amber put her hands on her hips, frowning at the blue-haired man. "It is? I think I'll have something to say about that."

Izban sighed. "You don't know them. We don't owe them anything; it was me who tracked you here. Let's go back to the school and forget this all happened."

"Forget?!" Amber shrieked angrily. "I've been tortured. I've been hurt. A part of me still wants to attack Macey because of what the Voice showed me. I won't be able to forget this. Ever. So, if you want to go, fine, but rest assured you'll never see me again."

Izban stared at her, speechless. Inside, Macey applauded her. Despite her youthful looks and her current weak condition, she'd told him off in the most magnificent way. She was making notes for future uses.

"Now, I'm going to go back in there," Amber continued. "I'm no longer alone and I'm no longer bound. We can fight him together. There's no point in leaving now while we're already here."

SO CONFIDENT. IT'S GOING TO BE HEARTBREAKING ONCE YOU REALISE THAT YOU'VE NEVER LEFT.

Suddenly, the world evaporated. It was like the people around Macey suddenly dissolved into mist and drifted away, leaving her alone. Well, not quite alone.

Amber was by her side. There was nothing else. Not even colour. They were standing on a white floor, but there were no walls, no nothing. Just endless whiteness.

"Amber?" Macey asked carefully, "Are you seeing the same?"

"If you mean a lot of white, then yes. And no Izban." Her voice was quivering slightly.

THE NEXT TIME YOU'LL SEE HIM WILL BE ON THE DAY OF YOUR DEATH.

"Stop being so dramatic!" Macey shouted, trying to convince both herself and Amber that they needn't be afraid.

The Voice ignored her.

LET'S CONTINUE WHERE WE LEFT OFF EARLIER.

Mist drifted into the air around them, forming shapes and colours, until they were suddenly back in the courtyard where Macey had first laid eyes upon

Amber. She still didn't know what that girl was, except that she was strong. Incredibly strong.

"I will get out of here, I will get out of here," Amber began to whisper, a desperate mantra. "I will get out of here. I will..."

YOU WON'T. NEITHER WILL YOU, LITTLE KELPIE.

Without warning, they were ripped apart, flying through the air until they landed roughly on opposite ends of the courtyard. Ignoring the pain in her limbs, Macey jumped to her feet. She could guess what the Voice was planning next.

BEITHIR. KILL HER.

A beithir! Finally, Macey knew what Amber was. And it scared her a little. She didn't know a lot about beithirs except that they could kill in a variety of ways. Their fangs were poisonous, they could control the weather, they could fly and attack you from above. When they shifted, of course. So far, Amber had stayed human, which is why Macey hadn't figured out her species before. It was hard not to recognise a shifted beithir... there weren't any other supernaturals that looked like a giant snake.

Amber was still on the ground, weakly trying to get to her feet. She'd expended too much energy; she wasn't going to be much of a threat.

But... when had reality been taken over by the Voice? Had it been after Amber attacked Macey with lightning? Or before? If it was before... then Amber would still have enough power to do another such attack. And Macey wasn't sure if she could escape her fate a second time. Had the Voice let them play out their battle in their minds so he could see what was going to happen? Did he want to see how they would escape so he could prevent it from ever happening?

Macey shivered. How was she supposed to fight someone who could play with her perception of what was real and what wasn't? She was still having trouble believing that she hadn't just spoken to her men. Were they really coming for her? Was Izban actually able to do a tracking spell, or had that bit been Amber's wishful thinking?

KILL HER, the Voice repeated and this time, Amber was magically dragged onto her feet by an unseen force. She wavered, but somehow managed to stand. Tiny sparks of lightning began to flicker around the girl's fingers and Macey prepared for the inevitable.

But wait... she was no longer wearing the copper cuffs. That had to mean that the battle had taken place and their combined power had opened them.

Was the Voice aware of that? Did he want an execution or a cat fight?

Amber opened her mouth, but Macey couldn't hear what she was saying. They were too far apart. Well, that could be rectified.

Macey carefully walked towards Amber, aware that there might be a dangerous surprise waiting at every step. Earlier, there'd been guards lying dead or unconscious all over the courtyard. This time, they were alone.

She shook her head in confusion. There was no way of telling what was real and what wasn't. Maybe she was still in her cell. Maybe she'd never even met Amber and this was all one giant illusion.

Suddenly, the air in front of her flickered and someone appeared. Someone very familiar with very blue hair.

Izban.

KILL HER OR I WILL KILL HIM.

Amber's eyes widened as she saw her friend. He didn't move; he seemed more statue than living being. Macey walked around him and took a closer look.

His eyes were moving but the rest of him wasn't. His face was an expressionless mask, but his eyes told her of his fear.

She could almost believe that he was real. That he was in danger.

A lightning bolt hit the ground next to her and she jumped back in surprise. Amber seemed to be convinced that Izban was real.

Another bolt of lightning crashed down at Macey's side, and she almost jumped back. If she was going to have Amber around, then she'd probably better get used to having this happen.

"Amber," she tried to whisper, but her voice was hoarse, as if from a lack of water. That was odd. Unless there were other side effects of the visions the Voice had given them.

There wasn't any answer.

Macey steeled herself, then waved her hand through Izban's still form, completely unsurprised when her hand passed right through him. Another visual trick then.

"Amber, please," she shouted, the wind that was beginning to rage stealing her words. Potentially the other woman's doing too. She'd heard that beithirs were storm creatures, not just lightning ones. "He's not real."

Her words weren't having any effect, and one look at the redhead revealed just how bad things were. Her eyes had taken on a crazed look, and there was no doubt about how mad the woman was.

"AMBER!" she shouted even louder, but again, no response.

Sucking in a deep breath, she did the only thing she could think of, and unleashed a ball of water at the girl.

A sharp squeal, followed by a calming in the winds, told her the trick had worked even better than she'd intended.

"What did you do that for?" Amber shouted, venom almost as poisonous as her fangs dripping from her tone.

"He's not real," Macey said softly, ignoring the glares she received in return. "Look." She passed her hand through the still form of the blue-haired man, and Amber's green eyes widened.

"How do I know he's not trapped somewhere here?" Her voice cracked as she spoke, and Macey's heart went out to her. She felt the same way when she thought of her own men in danger, so there was very little doubt in her mind how Amber felt about Izban.

Good job he seemed to feel the same.

"Because I was with him before I was taken," she replied softly, hoping the Voice wouldn't be able to hear her whispers, but knowing that hope was likely in vain.

"You were?" Amber perked up at that, and Macey smiled.

"Yes. He was trying to find you."

I SAID TO KILL HER.

Amber sighed. "He's so demanding," she tried to joke.

"And throws a lot of tantrums," Macey added.

"What do we do now?"

"I suppose you try and kill me."

Maybe not her best idea, but they at least had to pretend for the moment.

"That seems a little counterproductive."

Macey cracked a smile. She could get used to having Amber around if she was going to make comments like that.

"Just while we think of an actual plan."

This time, Amber nodded. "Okay, sounds like the best idea we have."

"Which isn't saying a lot."

The red-head laughed. "No, it really doesn't."

She took two steps back and squared off against Macey, pushing her sleeves up and readying herself.

"Prepare to die, bitch," Amber taunted.

"Bring it on," Macey replied, unable to help the amused smile tugging at her lips. When she knew the other woman wasn't actually going to be aiming for her, she kind of looked forward to facing off against her. It was just an intense kind of training really. Her men would be happy.

Amber struck first, sending twin bolts of lightning either side of Macey.

Not waiting another moment, Macey summoned mini balls of water, and began juggling them in the air to gain momentum. Then, one after the other, she began to fling them at Amber, making sure each one narrowly missed the girl's head. Though one did accidentally come too close, luckily, Amber was quick enough to avoid it.

She must be running on adrenaline though. She'd

been weak to start with and could only be getting worse by the second.

Maybe that was the Voice's plan. To wear them out to the point where they were no longer able to even think of fighting back. That way, their minds would be easy to slip into, and he could take whatever control he wanted.

Wasn't that a cheery thought?

The two women danced around each other, flinging their powers back and forth with increasing ferocity. It was almost a battle of who could conjure the most elaborate piece of magic.

So far, Amber was winning. She'd conjured a massive snake, that probably looked something like her in shifted form, and made it coil around Macey. Being inside the electricity had been invigorating, and all she'd been able to see were the bright sparks coming off it.

Once the snake's coils had receded, she caught Amber's eye, trying to ensure the woman would do exactly the same again. Only this time, Macey would add to the power and do.... something. She wasn't all that sure what, but it was worth a shot.

"When you two are quite done, how about we actually consider getting you out of here?" a soft female voice sounded.

Macey whipped her head around in shock, and was surprised to see a petite woman, even smaller than she was, standing in an archway off the courtyard.

The woman's long mouse brown hair blew in the soft breeze, and her big eyes looked at the two of the scornfully.

"Who are you?" Macey asked, not letting her on guard posture go slack. For all she knew, this woman could be another trick on the part of the Voice, and she wasn't ready to relax on the off chance.

"Don't you recognise me, kelpie? I'm hurt. We had so many stellar conversations in your cell."

"Luch?" Macey's brows furrowed. She'd been under the impression that the mouse was male. In fact..."But you're a woman?"

"Well noticed. I can choose how I appear."

"What are you?" she asked in awe, slightly confused by the whole situation.

"Just Luch."

"Luch!"

Amber came running and threw herself at the women, hugging her tight. "I knew you weren't just a mouse!"

"I'll pretend I didn't hear you call me 'just a mouse'," Luch chuckled, returning Amber's hug. "But could we leave now, please? Let's keep the hugging for later."

Macey was still a little skeptical. "You didn't want to help me before. What's changed?"

The woman shrugged. "I've seen you two fight. It seems you may actually have a chance in beating Mahoun. It's worth the trouble now."

That made sense. Before, Luch had only seen her as a prisoner, taunted by the Voice.

"Okay, how do we get out?"

"We fly," Luch said and pointed at Amber. "If our beithir here can carry her boyfriend, she can carry both of us."

"Now wait a minute," Amber protested. "First, he's not my boyfriend. Second, I can carry one of you, not two. And third, I've already tried flying out of here. It's impossible." She shuddered and Macey wondered what had happened. Had she tried to escape? Had the Voice punished her for it?

"Last time you didn't have me," Luch smiled. "And I'll travel in Macey's pocket, don't worry about that."

Without warning, she shrunk into a mouse. Yes, that's exactly what it looked like. As if she suddenly deflated and became tiny within the blink of an eye.

"What are you looking at!" the tiny Luch shouted at the two women. "Never seen a mouse shift before?"

Macey closed her mouth and decided to say nothing. Luch was weird even by supernatural standard.

"Why couldn't you fly away from this place?" she asked Amber instead.

"There was a barrier high up in the air. Hard like glass but invisible. I crashed into it and almost broke my neck. Just about managed to avoid falling, but it's clear that there's something protecting this place. I tried it one other time to explore how big this barrier is and if it goes all around the castle, but they caught me before I got far. After that I decided not to try again."

Her eyes took on a defeated look for a moment, but then she squared her shoulders.

"But Luch has been with me for so long, and if she says that we can fly out of here, then I believe her. Let's do this."

STOP TALKING AND START KILLING!

All three women ignored the Voice this time. He'd not made an appearance in person yet, and so far, he was staying out of their minds, so he wasn't worth wasting time on.

Amber quickly took off her ragged clothes and shifted in one fluid motion.

By the waves! Macey had thought that the rumours about beithirs were just exaggerations, but obviously they were true. Amber had turned into a massive - giant! - snake with a head like a dragon and two long tendrils hanging from her chin. Despite this kind-of-beard, she still looked feminine somehow. Macey shook her head in amazement. How could that thin, small girl suddenly turn into this gigantic form? Of course, she was a bit larger as a kelpie than as a human herself, but the difference wasn't as mind-blowing as in Amber's case.

Strangely enough though, the beithir had no wings. How was she supposed to be able to fly?

Amber flicked her head, motioning Macey to get on her back.

She picked up little Luch and carefully sat down on where she supposed Amber's shoulders were. The beithir's scales were soft and warm, not at all what Macey had expected.

"Where do you want to sit?" she asked Luch, but the mouse was already climbing out of Macey's hand and up her shirt. Her tiny claws hurt a little, but Macey knew better than to complain. When the mouse reached the shirt's neckline, she climbed inside, making herself comfortable between Macey's breasts.

"Seriously?"

Luch snickered. "It's not my fault you don't have any pockets. Now fly, Amber, or we'll never make it out of here."

Amber nodded her massive head and tensed her muscles. Then they were up in the air, hovering above the ground. It looked effortless, as if gravity had decided to no longer work on the beithir. Amber wasn't even moving but still, she was flying. How very strange. Macey made a mental note to ask the girl later on how she did it.

They gently rose higher, increasing in speed. The courtyard below became smaller and smaller and Macey got a better view of the castle she'd been held prisoner in. It was a massive, expansive structure with dozens of towers and turrets. It had seen better times and on one side, the main wall was crumbling and some of the buildings had lost their roofs. It fit the image in her head that not many people actually lived here. It was just the Voice, the prisoners and some guards. There was smoke coming from a chimney on the main building in the centre of the castle, but that was the only sign of life.

Macey wondered where this castle was. Somewhere in Scotland? Elsewhere in Britain? Or maybe in a strange inbetween place like her men's house? There was a lot of mist all around them, covering the land surrounding the castle, but that could have been just the weather rather than the mists of the Staran. She supposed she was going to find out soon.

"Don't go too high, aim for that reddish tower over there!" Luch shouted and Amber nodded slightly to signal that she'd heard.

While most of the castle was built from dark grey stone, there was one sandstone tower that they were now flying towards. It looked almost too pretty to be in a place like this.

"There's a hole in the barrier just above the merlons that you should be able to squeeze through."

"Should?" Macey shouted against the wind. "Are you sure we're going to fit?"

"I didn't think she'd be this big!" Luch shouted back. "We'll see!"

Macey's hair whipped around her face. She really should have learned from last time to carry hair ties with her. Advice for another time. It wasn't like she could do anything about it right this second.

She couldn't do much about anything.

Luch squeaked from between her breasts, clearly enjoying the experience. Why wasn't Macey surprised? The mouse was an odd creature indeed.

She wasn't sure what made her do it, but Macey ducked down and pressed her body flush against Amber's smooth scales. A static charge started to build around her body, and she tried to brush it off. An undercurrent of concern remained. She didn't want this to end badly, otherwise the three of them could end up trapped with only the Voice as company again.

Or at least, Macey and Amber would. Luch could probably come and go as she pleased. Then again, there must be a way that the mouse was shielding her mind. Otherwise the Voice would have already known about the creature, and done something about it. Macey didn't think it'd be likely for him to leave anyone alone who was already within his clutches.

The static built more, causing Macey's ears to pop. She held back a groan. That was never a good feeling, and in her weak state, it was even worse. If they failed in their attempt to escape, then there was a good chance she wouldn't be able to fight in the state she was in. Weakened and disheartened. To say the least.

Amber likely wasn't that much better. Though using her power did seem to have restored her a little bit.

Surprisingly, Macey recognised the moment they flew through the hole in the barrier. It was almost as if something scraped across her skin. But Amber was flexible in this form, and while it was slow going, she did manage to twist and turn her way through.

It wasn't until fresh air hit Macey's face that she actually breathed a sigh of relief. As with their fake escape, she could feel the difference between this air, and the air from within the Voice's fort. It was stale in there, probably a result of so many prisoners.

Though the comparison did nothing for the lingering worry that they hadn't actually escaped, and that this was just another trick of the Voice's. In fact, if he hadn't been such a show off, Macey might even have wondered if Luch was the Voice, and just taking another form to mess with them.

Mind games. It was all just mind games. Which scared her. Physically, she was powerful, and strong. She could fight something if she could see it and she had to. But mentally? Macey wasn't so sure. Especially given the events of the past weeks. There was no doubting she wasn't as strong as she thought she was. Not by any stretch of anyone's imagination. Which was a shame. She had to make sure her brothers never heard her admit that.

Her brothers...

She'd left them in there. If that was even them.

But no. She couldn't think about them right now. There was nothing she could do while so high in the air. And there was nothing she could do without risking all three of their lives. If it was just her going back in there, then she could have accepted it. But it wasn't. Neither Amber or Luch deserved the extra danger in their lives. If Macey could keep them far away from here, then that would be the best course of action.

Though she doubted it was going to be as simple as that for Amber. The other woman, or the giant flying snake, depending on what form she was in, was the Lightning Warden, after all. At least, Macey doubted anyone else could have given her a mark. Which meant that Amber was stuck with her for now.

From what she'd seen of the red-head, she didn't

think there'd be any qualms on her part for seeing this thing through.

Izban was going to be another matter. There was something deep down that told her he was going to be a problem. Even if it was just a slightly argumentative one. Hopefully her men had got him into a more supportive state in the time they'd all been a part.

She made a mental note to try and work out just how long that had actually been. It was an almost certainty that she'd been away from her men for a longer amount of time than they'd been together, and she just hoped they hadn't forgotten about her.

Macey chastised herself. Of course, they hadn't forgotten her. Cam would never let them forget their jobs as Wardens for a start. Flint just wouldn't want to let her go. And Jared...

Shit. Jared. He might not be doing so well if she'd been away for more than a few days. He'd said his incubus was more under control when she was near, which meant that now she wasn't...probably best she didn't go there.

A jolt shook her from her thoughts, and she glanced around, slightly surprised to see the light dimming around them already.

The second jolt was all it took Macey to figure out Amber was becoming too tired to fly. Really, they should all be amazed they'd gotten this far without falling out of the sky. It said a lot about the beithir's mental strength and sheer determination.

"I think it's time to rest," Macey shouted over the wind, only to have the large snake nod its head.

Luch shuffled a little inside her shirt, but didn't pop her head out, meaning the mouse was probably asleep. Lucky for her.

Macey's eyes were beginning to droop, and she imagined Amber's were doing the same. They had to be. Flying felt like draining business.

The next time they lost height, it was a much smoother process, suggesting that Amber was doing it on purpose this time. Macey appreciated the softer flight pattern. Almost as much as she'd appreciate solid ground.

Ceasg

4

This time, there were no men awaiting them. Macey was quite glad, actually, because she wasn't sure if she could have believed them to be real. It was all so confusing. She didn't want to hug and kiss them if they were only figments of her imagination. Or the Voice's imagination. She shuddered as she tried to find a more comfortable place on the ground. Something was digging into her hips, but no matter how she turned and tossed, there was always a place that hurt or pricked or annoyed her. Sleeping on the ground wasn't comfortable, and even though she knew she needed to sleep to recharge her energy, she was having a hard time actually doing so.

Luch apparently didn't. The tiny mouse was snoring as loud as a human, nestled against Amber's chin. The girl had decided to stay in her beithir form for protection and warmth, and Macey was a little jealous of her. She'd probably be more comfortable in her kelpie form as well, but for that, she needed water or she'd suffocate. So here she was, fighting to sleep.

They'd talked about one of them staying up to keep watch, but all three of them were too tired so they'd scrapped that plan. If anyone wanted to attack them, they were too weak to fight much anyway. Especially if the Voice decided to show up.

Macey checked that her mental barriers were still in place. Thank the waves, they were. She thought they might have become a little stronger since she got Amber's lightning mark, but maybe that was just wishful thinking. For now, the Voice hadn't tried and infiltrate her mind, so that was a good sign at least.

Unless this was all still one of his games.

Macey shuddered again. Her brothers would call it mindfuck, but as a princess, she'd not use such language. She'd only really learned swear words once she'd left the loch and moved to Earth. It had been an enlightening process. Humans had such a colourful language.

She turned again, this time because her thigh was pressed against something hard, probably a small stone. This night was going to be long and uncomfortable.

EVENTUALLY, she must have fallen asleep because waking up was a long and painful process, despite the little claws tapping her cheeks.

"Luch, stop it," she groaned, tempted to pull her non-existent blanket over her face.

"Rise and shine," the mouse said cheerily, continuing to pat Macey's face with her paws. "Come on, we need to leave and get some distance between us and him."

That woke Macey up. The Voice. Yes, they needed to leave and get away. And hopefully find her men in the process.

She sat up and saw a very human Amber crouching in a bush not far away. Macey averted her gaze, not wanting to intrude into the other woman's privacy. Her own bladder was telling her it was time for a potty break as well. At the same time, she was thirsty. They needed to find themselves some water and food soon.

She rubbed the sleep from her eyes and looked around. Last night, it had been dark and hard to see where exactly they'd landed. Now, she was glad they hadn't. It was too depressing.

They were in a barren, brown landscape full of mud, low hills and thorny shrubs. No houses, no signs of life. Not even a single tree. And no colours, either.

A hundred shades of brown and grey, but nothing living. She looked at the ground. No grass, either. Just mud and fallen leaves.

Wait, leaves? How could there be leaves without trees?

Please, don't let this be another of the Voice's mind games.

The better option was that this was some kind of magical place. Like the Staran, but more depressing. Purgatory. Something like that. A place so hopeless and desolate that her heart sank with every minute she had to look at the dead landscape.

How were they going to find food here? And water?

The mud was wet, so maybe it rained here occasionally, but for now, she was more interested in a stream or loch.

She got up and patted down her clothes, glad she'd been lying on leaves rather than mud. Amber returned from behind the bush and gave Macey a small smile.

"Good morning. Not the nicest place we've ended up in."

Macey grimaced. "You could say that. Any idea what direction we came from?"

Amber pointed to her left. "That way. And I'd be tempted to just fly into the other direction. All I want is to get away from him."

"So, we're going to fly again? Are you feeling strong enough?"

Amber smiled. "I'm feeling like a new beithir. Let's see if we can find a way out of this place. Ready?"

She sounded excited. After being in captivity for so long, even being in this dreich place had to be exhilarating for the redhead.

"Yes, I'm ready. Stop ignoring me," Luch peeped and stamped her tiny paw.

Macey suppressed a snort. The mouse was hilarious, no matter how serious she was trying to be. Luckily, she hadn't changed back to a woman though. Macey had found that a little unnerving. Somehow, she didn't believe Luch was just a simple mouse shifter.

Amber shifted in one fluid motion and beckoned them to get on her back. Macey picked up Luch and put her back into her cleavage. Luch moved around a little until she found the perfect position: her front paws hanging onto the rim of Macey's shirt and her head sticking out so she could see what was going on.

Lucky Luch, she was probably going to feel nice and cosy in there. Macey shivered. It was cold in this place, and steam was beginning to rise from the muddy ground. Yes, it was time to leave.

She sat down on Amber's back, now more aware of the most comfortable and safe position.

"Ready!" she called and Amber began to fly.

They gained height quickly, giving them a better view of where they were. Except that there was nothing to see. Endless desolate plains with no signs of life. Not even a ruin that would show that people once lived here.

They flew for hours until Macey was shivering uncontrollably from the harsh cold wind they were exposed to this high in the air.

"Can we take a break?" she finally asked when she was beginning to have trouble holding on to the beithir. Amber's scales were warm, but it wasn't enough to stop Macey from feeling terribly cold.

Amber nodded and began to descend. She didn't seem exhausted at all, and Macey was a little jealous. She was feeling tired, thirsty and hungry, and just wanted to curl up in a ball and be miserable.

With a sigh of relief, Macey climbed off Amber's back and jumped up and down a little, getting some warmth into her frozen limbs. Her thighs hurt from holding on to the large beithir for so long. She'd never ridden a horse before but somehow imagined it might feel similar.

Suddenly, a scent hit her nose, a very familiar one. She breathed in deeply and smiled.

"I can smell water!"

She began to follow the scent, half-walking, half-running over the muddy ground. Her feet made squelchy sounds with every step; it was weird being on such soft ground.

About a hundred metres away, she found it. A tiny stream. The water was a yellowish brown, but it smelled drinkable. Water was Macey's element and her nose told her that this stream was safe. And even better, it led to a large pool.

Finally, a good thing was happening to them. Things were beginning to look up.

The water called to her. As it always did. It'd been too long since her dip in her men's swimming pool.

Next to her, Amber started humming, now back in human form. She meandered towards the murky pool of water, not seeming to have a care in the world.

"Amber?" Macey asked carefully, starting to worry about how zoned out the beithir looked. That couldn't be normal. "Amber?" she repeated louder, still not getting any response.

Luch squeaked from her position between Macey's boobs, and used her paws to tug down the material of her shirt. Macey assumed it was to have a better look, though she wished the mouse wouldn't do that, it left her feeling all kinds of exposed.

"Uh-oh, that's not good," Luch said.

"You don't say," Macey deadpanned, before taking a couple of steps forward, hoping to reach the other woman and pull her away from the water. Something clearly wasn't right. Especially for the pull towards it to have suddenly turned into an urge to get them all away from it. Something about it felt off, and it wasn't the murky colouration. Macey was well aware that even the dirtiest looking water wasn't always so. It could just have been a certain kind of algae that was making it like that.

She took another step, and ground to a halt, something stopping her from moving any further forward, almost like the barrier that had stopped them from leaving the Voice's keep. She tried again, to no avail.

"Want to try?" she asked the mouse.

She felt it nod against her skin, but the sensation only lasted for a moment. Luch leaped from her shirt, shifting as she did, only to be replaced by the same woman as before. It surprised Macey, she'd half expected Luch to appear differently again.

The mouse took a few steps forward and came against the same problem Macey had. Not a good sign in the slightest.

"That's a no go, then."

"What do we do now?" Macey asked, worry building within her.

Amber had reached the edge of the water now and hadn't seemed to rouse from her spaced out state. That couldn't be good at all. Macey didn't know if beithirs could breathe underwater, though she suspected they couldn't. And if the red-head carried on, then she was going to risk drowning. There was very little doubt there.

The water was now lapping around Amber's legs, but she didn't even seem to notice. Macey's concern grew worse. This certainly wasn't a good thing. It was almost as bad as when the Voice took control of people. At least, from what she'd seen.

A ripple in the pool of the water drew her attention away from the beithir, and to her surprise, a head poked up above the calm surface. It only appeared for a moment, but there was no mistaking what it was. The woman had dark green hair that floated around the surface. Her skin was a similar hue, and if Macey's eyes hadn't been as strong as they were, then she probably wouldn't have noticed her. The skin and hair clearly matched the colour of the pool and must have been designed for camouflage.

Macey wracked her brain for the knowledge of other water beings that her Aunt Nessie had imparted in her, but it was hard to tell without seeing the woman's entire body. For all Macey knew, she could be yet another kind of kelpie. Even though she'd been led to believe her family was the only kind, the storm kelpies had thrown that idea out of the window.

"She doesn't look very friendly," Luch said.

"The teeth?" Macey half-joked, though her voice

was shaking. She pushed against the barrier again, trying her best to get past it, but it still wouldn't budge.

A splash drew her attention, and a thick tail, not unlike the salmon that passed through the rivers near her loch, disappeared into the lake.

Realisation crashed through her, and she renewed her efforts to get through the barrier. A ceasg was bad news. Very bad news. Especially for Amber, who was now chest deep in the water and only getting closer to the creature. Macey had heard a lot of stories about the creatures, some of which involved them eating people whole and keeping them in their stomachs for years.

That couldn't happen.

Not only did Macey need the other woman for their fight to save the Staran, but she'd come to like her in the short time since they'd met.

"Shit!" she shouted, as she bounced back past the barrier again.

"I have something I can try," Luch said softly. "But you're going to have to trust me."

"Anything." Tears stung Macey's eyes as she agreed, and Luch nodded her head. Right now, her only focus was on making sure Amber was safe.

"I need you to be ready to run for the water and shift as soon as this works," Luch instructed.

"Okay," Macey agreed shakily, wondering what was about to happen.

"I don't know if this will hurt or not, but if it does, I'm sorry," the mouse added, before lifting her hands and cupping them together.

An intense look of concentration covered Luch's face, and a tugging sensation built within Macey, as if someone was drawing on her power. She opened her mouth to speak, but Luch shook her head, stopping her in her tracks.

Instead, she looked at Amber in the water. She was still walking into the centre of the pool, but it didn't look to have gotten much deeper. The beithir's tail twitched from where it floated in the water, and hope rose instead. Until she realised that was Luch's doing too.

Something swirled around the woman's hand, and before long, lightning and water were swirling there, much like they had when Amber and Macey had combined their powers earlier.

With a deep breath, Luch threw the power in the direction of the barrier. It lit up as the lightning crackled around it, before disappearing in the blink of an eye.

Macey stood there for a few gob smacked moments, before realising what she should be doing.

Without waiting a second longer, she began to run towards the lake, already pulling on a shift, knowing she'd hit the water before she needed to breathe.

Even with her kelpie vision, it was hard to see underwater. Amber walking into the pool had whirled up a lot of mud which was now threatening to clog up Macey's eyes. The water was a lot deeper than she'd thought, deep enough for several kelpies to stand on top of each other. She was by Amber's side in a flash, using her powerful tail to propel her forwards.

She took a deep breath and broke the surface to check what the other woman was doing. Amber stared blankly into the distance, but she'd stopped moving. She was now to her neck in water but didn't seem to be bothered by it in the slightest.

Macey couldn't speak so she whinnied loudly, but Amber didn't even blink. She was in a deep trance, but how to get her out of it?

Macey went back underwater to check for the strange woman she'd seen earlier. She'd never heard anything good about the ceasg, but she had to keep reminding herself that most people thought kelpies were monsters, too. So, she should really keep an open mind... but luring Amber into the water like that wasn't a good sign.

She came to a halt and listened. The water around her was flowing steadily, a rhythm that she could focus on. Now if there was to be a disturbance to the rhythm... yes, there it was! She shot towards her target and almost crashed into the ceasg.

The woman was swimming close to the surface, a few metres downstream from Amber. If you ignored her sharp teeth and strange colour, she could almost be called beautiful. No wonder there were stories of human men falling in love with these river mermaids. She smiled toothily at Macey, who wasn't quite sure what to do. Could she communicate with this other species?

Kelpies used language that to humans sounded like whinnies and dolphin-like clicks. So far, she'd not met anyone other than kelpies who could understand it. And most other supernaturals made fun of it because it sounded so unsophisticated. They just didn't understand the nuances of a well-executed click.

"Who are you?" she asked in her own language, not really expecting a response.

I am Mhara.

Ah, she was one of those mind-talkers. Not everybody could talk in the pretty sounds of the kelpie.

"What do you want from my friend, Mhara?"

I was curious. I've not come across someone like her before.

"So, you entranced her to walk into the water just to satisfy your curiosity?"

Pretty much, yes. But why are you here, kelpie? I've only ever met one of you before. He was quite a bore.

"We were just passing through," Macey said noncommittally. She still didn't know if this Mhara was friend or foe.

"Now that you've seen her, could you let Amber go, please, so we can move on?"

Tell me first, what is she?

Macey wasn't sure if she should divulge Amber's identity, but at the same time, what could it hurt?

"She's a shifter. A beithir."

Oh, I've not met one of those before. Do they taste good?

Macey immediately shifted her position, making herself big and threatening. The ceasg was getting nowhere near her new friend.

Stop it, that was a joke! Seems you've heard the same rumours as everybody else has. She scratched her chin. *I'm sure it's the selkies who've been spreading that nonsense.*

"Yes, I suppose they may have," Macey said weakly, a bit embarrassed that she'd reacted the same way to the ceasg as everybody else reacted to kelpies.

We're not bad people. We're actually quite useful, if one asks us nicely.

"Why, what can you do?"

You've not heard of the maidens of the water granting wishes to all who capture us? Now, I'd like you not to imprison me, please, but I am able to grant you one wish.

"Ehm, that's nice of you," Macey spluttered. This

woman was weird. "We never really planned to be here... Can you bring us back to Earth?"

Earth is a big place, my dear. Where exactly would you like to be?

Macey thought back to a vision the Voice gave her long ago. Maybe it was time to turn it into reality.

It was time to visit Aunt Nessie.

5

A kelpie, a mouse and a beithir walked into a bar. There was almost nobody in the pub, only a tired looking landlord leaning against a large cask of ale, and a few older customers playing chess in a corner. They ignored the three young women, probably mistaking them for tourists.

Macey headed straight to the pub owner. She'd seen him once before, but that was ages ago and she doubted he'd remember her.

"I'm looking for Nessie, have you seen her?"

He stared at her before breaking into roaring laughter. "Dearie, aren't ye a bit too old to believe in Nessie?"

Macey crossed her arms in front of her chest. "She's my aunt." She lowered her voice. "And I know she's a kelpie and comes here several times a week. So, tell me, do you know if she'll be here today?"

The man looked at her for a moment, then nodded.

"There's a pub quiz tonight that she usually comes to. It's still a few hours to go until then, though. Want some scran?"

"Scran?"

Macey could hear the disgust in Luch's voice but ignored it. It was almost unfortunate that she was in human form, that way people could actually hear her. Then again, she was certain the pub landlord wasn't human. There was no other way he'd have been so unconcerned with her mention of kelpies.

As always, Macey's mind started racing a mile a minute trying to work out *what* he was.

"Ignore her. Three of whatever's on offer," she said with a smile. "But I'm vegetarian."

"Just like your Aunt."

Macey smiled at him a little uneasily. Maybe this wasn't quite the best of ideas. But the ceasg hadn't been able to transport her to her men. Apparently, people were harder to find than places, and without even a general idea, there'd been nowhere to send the three women.

"Yes," she said weakly.

"I'll serve you in the backroom. There's someone in there who'll want to see you."

Dread filled her. Those weren't the kind of words she ever wanted to hear from anyone. Especially when they were effectively on the run from their captor.

"Don't look so worried, Malan sent them to you."

"How did he-"

"If you've forgotten his powers already, then we have bigger problems than if you'll go into the back-room now," the Landlord answered, chuckling away to himself.

Macey wouldn't admit to being happy. She didn't think she'd be happy if she was sat at a banquet table with all three of her men and a mountain of waffles with all the trimmings. After the adventure she'd been having, she deserved all the whipped cream, strawberries and chocolate sauce she could get her hands on.

"Who is Malan?" Amber whispered, but Macey just shook her head.

The conversation of exactly who, and what, the headless prophet was, would take far too long.

"Very well," Macey replied, ignoring the small squeak of protest from Luch. She had no say here either. Macey wasn't even sure why the mouse was still with them, or what her agenda was. While she wanted to believe she had decent motives, and she certainly did seem to be good friends with Amber, nothing was ever certain in this world.

For all Macey knew, Luch was just the Voice playing with them in a different form. Though something deep in her gut had her sure that wasn't the case. And if there was one thing she needed to trust more, it was her own instincts. Ignoring them seemed to constantly get her into trouble.

The landlord waved them towards a dim doorway to the side of the bar, and Macey sighed. She'd really been looking forward to having some downtime. And a pub quiz had sounded kind of perfect, even if she would struggle without someone who'd lived on earth longer than she had.

Pushing through the door, a dimly lit room was revealed. Almost like the kind she'd expect to find in a fantasy film. A heavy wooden table dominated the centre of the room, with uncomfortable looking chairs around the edge of it.

None of them were filled.

So much for someone wanting to see them.

"Welcome, kelpie, beithir, Luch," an ethereal voice said.

Macey looked around frantically, trying to work out where it had come from. Oddly, she found nothing.

"Hi?" she called out into the room.

A shriek sounded from Amber, and Macey turned on her heels to see what the matter was. To her surprise, a woman's form was floating in front of her.

Only, she wasn't completely a woman. She was translucent, much like Malan had been. Though at least *this* person had a body. It was far less disconcerting than chatting with a floating head.

"Hello, Macey," the woman replied.

"How do you know my name?" she asked, already filled with a little trepidation.

"Malan sent me. But I knew it anyway. You are part of a prophecy after all." The woman's voice echoed around the room, with a breathy quality that made it all the more otherworldly.

"Ah, yes. How is Malan?" she asked, trying to be polite. While the situation might be unorthodox, she refused to forget her manners.

"Bodiless, as always." The spirit laughed, and Macey really didn't know how to take that. She wasn't used to dead people being so amusing.

"Do you have a name?" Macey walked further into a room and sat herself on one of the uncomfortable looking chairs. They had high backs at least, and she slumped into it, enjoying the rest for the first time since before being captured by the Voice.

It took Luch and Amber another moment, but they soon followed, taking seats either side of her, and leaving the other side for the spirit woman.

"Of course. How rude of me. I'm Fedelm."

"And you're human?" Amber asked, not taking her eyes off the woman.

"No, I'm dead."

"Sorry, *were* you a human?" Amber rephrased.

The beithir didn't seem in the least bit concerned that they were talking to a ghost. Macey made a note to ask her about that later. There must be something more to the acceptance than just an open mind.

"Of a kind. I believe there's some sìth blood in my family line. But I was born human. I'm more known for my predictions for Queen Medb."

"It's a long way from Ireland," Luch said, studying her nails with an amused glint in her eye.

"Isn't it a long way from where you truly live, little mouse?"

Luch looked up sharply. Macey had no idea what that was about, but let it lie for now. She didn't want to cause any tension between her and her new ally.

"The Staran and the Wardens are hardly just confined to Scotland. People the world over are at risk if they're destroyed. Ireland really isn't that far to come. Plus, they're not exactly my biggest fans over there."

"What did you do?" Macey asked, intrigued.

"Predicted blood and destruction. People always like to know the warnings, but when they don't listen, and you're right, they hate you for it."

"I'm sorry," Macey responded.

"That can't have been easy," Amber added, her tail twitching where she'd placed it over her lap. Macey had an odd urge to reach out and touch it, but only so she could see how it felt. She wondered if it'd be the same as Amber's scales in shifted form, or if it'd be softer, like skin.

"Crimson-red from blood they are; I behold them bathed in red, " Luch recited softly. "Did you really say that or is that just the legend?"

Fedelm laughed. "I can't even remember. It's a long time ago. And it's not why I'm here now. Malan knew you'd come here, but he didn't know when." She sighs. "He's never been good at predicting times. I've been waiting here for week, and-"

"Wait, I've been gone for weeks?" Macey interrupted, her voice shrill. "That can't be right, it's not been that long. Maybe two weeks at most, right?"

She looked questioningly at Amber, but the beithir only shrugged. "I could have been there for years and I wouldn't know. He twists your mind and memories until you can no longer tell apart present, past and future."

Fedelm nodded sagely. "Time passes differently in different places. I believe it's been two months since you were taken. It's been incredibly boring, there's nothing to do in this village. Your aunt and the pub quizzes are the only entertainment, and those are not even every evening. I'll be glad to get away from here." She huffed. "I wish Malan would have done this himself, but he doesn't blend in as nicely as I do."

Amber snickered and even Luch laughed loudly, much louder than a mouse should be able to.

Fedelm pointed down at her translucent body. "This is much better than being a floating head, right?"

Macey nodded quickly, hoping the woman would get to the point. Knowing she'd been away for so long, she was beginning to panic a little, and was hoping Fedelm would be able to distract her. Give them some good news, even.

"Anyway, Malan would like you to know that it's no longer safe to travel on the Staran without a wraith or ghost. Even the na fir ghorma no longer have access to them. If you'd try to travel on them, it would likely tear you apart. Which means you'll have to wait for your men to come to you. How do you feel about several weeks of pub quizzes?"

Macey stared at her in shock. "Wait, we're stuck here?"

"Yup," the prophet said simply. "Maybe use the time to figure out how to save the world? You better hurry up, the Staran are getting worse by the day. And I believe you still have your seventh Warden to find."

Anger bubbled up in Macey. Fedelm made it sound so easy, as if all Macey had to do was put in a bit more effort. By the waves, she'd been held prisoner for several weeks, of course she hadn't had the time to do anything about the situation. Besides, all she had to go on was a vague prophecy. This really seemed hopeless. How can you fix something without knowing what's wrong?

"We're working on it," Amber said diplomatically, a lot calmer than Macey felt. "I don't suppose you know where our men... ehm, friends are?"

"I do, actually. They're my next stop... I just have to decide how quickly to start looking for them."

Macey frowned. "What's stopping you?"

A silver sheen crept over Fedelm's cheeks. Was the ghost blushing?

"Well, I've always wanted to meet the famous Nessie, but so far, she's been ignoring me. If you could introduce me, I'm sure I could find your men a lot quicker."

"That's blackmail!"

The woman chuckled. "No, it's curiosity. Come on, it's only a few extra hours. I promise I'll bring your men to you straight after. Deal?"

Macey looked at Amber, who shrugged in bewilderment.

The kelpie sighed. "Let's hope my aunt arrives soon."

Luckily, they only needed to wait for an hour before Nessie arrived. They used the time to have some food and warm themselves by the fire. Somehow, Macey could still feel the cold of their long flight in her bones.

Fedelm had taken on an even more translucent shape and had reassured them that none of the humans would be able to see them. Not everyone here knew about Nessie and the supernatural world, and they wanted to keep it that way.

The ghost seemed to be enjoying their company immensely and was quizzing them about their love lives. Somehow, Macey felt as if she was back at school among gossiping teenage girls.

"So how did you meet your boy?" Fedelm asked Amber and the beithir smiled in embarrassment.

"He was a teacher, no, he pretended to be a teacher at my school."

"To woo you? Oh, how romantic!" The ghost clapped her hands excitedly.

Amber laughed. "No, he was actually on a mission to find some items that were hidden at the school. I ended up helping him find them and then... well, we kind of destroyed them."

Fedelm looked just as confused as Macey felt. "Wait, you found something and then destroyed it? That doesn't make sense."

"It's a long story," the beithir sighed. "It turned

out that Izban's grandfather wanted them to make himself immortal. We didn't think that was a good idea, so we decided to stop him."

"Did it work?"

"I was taken by Mahoun before I could find out. I hope so, although I'm sure an immortal mage is the least of our worries."

"Damn right," a deep, sultry voice said behind them and Macey turned around in delight.

"Auntie Nessie!"

She hugged her aunt before the old kelpie took a seat between Macey and Amber.

Fedelm seemed frozen in awe, her eyes fixed on Nessie, her silver blush darkening her face.

"I've not seen you in a while, Macey dear," Aunt Nessie said while absentmindedly motioning for the bartender to bring her a drink. She was well known in here, they all knew what the old lady liked.

Macey had to stop herself from blurting out that it didn't feel all that long to her, having had a strange vision sent by a megalomaniac Voice. She didn't want to scare her aunt.

"How are you?" she asked instead, but her aunt tsked.

"Stop the small talk, that's not your style. Why are you here?"

Macey grinned. Her aunt's frankness was refreshing.

"Have you noticed anything strange recently? Like... ehm... wrongness?"

"Macey, just tell me what's going on."

The younger kelpie grimaced. "Basically, the world is ending and I'm part of a prophecy to prevent it from happening. But I'm not quite sure what to do and nobody is telling me and my men aren't here and I was a prisoner and..."

Her voice broke and a lone tear forced its way down Macey's cheek.

"Oh, my darling," Nessie huffed and took her niece into her arms. "Are you sure you're not over-reacting?"

Amber cleared her throat. "No, she isn't. And I'm Amber, by the way, and this is Fedelm."

"Goodness me, where are my manners," Nessie exclaimed, before smirking. "Oh, that's right, I don't have any. Lovely to meet you nonetheless."

"And this is Luch," Macey added, lifting her head up slightly as the sobs calmed.

The look on her Aunt's face was hard to define, all Macey knew was that she didn't like it. Aunt Nessie's face verged on distaste, and even if Macey was wary of the mouse, she'd proved herself to be more of a friend than a foe, and she didn't want to chase her away, particularly after her trick with the barrier. If they got into any other tight spots, then Luch was likely to be able to get them out.

"I am Nessie," her Aunt said, somewhat stiffly.

"And I am Luch," the mouse replied, a lot more jovially, as if making fun of the older woman. Macey would say it was a bad idea, but she really wasn't sure which of the two women was the most powerful. But she wasn't going to bring that up. Even if she had been able to get it out through the now drying tears.

"Pleasure." Aunt Nessie's voice dripped with sarcasm. If it had been one of her men being that way, then Macey would have told them off for being so rude. But when it came to Aunt Nessie, she was a little more hesitant. The woman was formidable, and in the Loch, she technically outranked her still. While the kelpies had a monarchy, there was some preference given towards power. One that meant Macey was well aware of the faction that wanted her on the throne over her brothers. She chose to ignore them. Causing dissent within the royal family was never the answer.

"I'll go get your men now," Fedelm said, floating nervously from side to side.

"Thank you," Macey replied, pushing herself away from the comfort of her Aunt's embrace. The emotion of the moment had been too much for her. But if she was going to lead the Wardens in their quest to save the world, then she needed to be strong. Which meant acting like the Princess she wanted to be, not the scared woman she really was at that moment.

"Men?" Aunt Nessie raised an eyebrow. "Is there something you need to tell me, Macey?" There was a slight accusation in her tone, as if Macey should have spilled the beans about her love life the moment her Aunt had entered the room.

Her cheeks heated and she wrung her hands together. She didn't really want to have this conversation. But it wasn't looking like there were many ways for her to avoid it.

"Yes, Auntie. Men. Three to be precise. Well, four. But one of them is Amber's."

"And the rest are yours?" Aunt Nessie asked, speaking over Amber's weak protest.

Macey didn't understand why the beithir was still denying what was between her and the Ice Warden. Even without seeing them together, she could tell just how enamored they were with one another. Thankfully, there was nothing like constant danger to bring people together. She'd be very surprised if the two of them weren't together by the end of their mission.

If they survived that was.

"Yes. Unless Cat-Man is still with them. Though I doubt he'll have stayed around for months while they searched for us."

"I'll take that as my cue to leave," Fedelm announced, before disappearing into a puff of mist.

Macey shuddered. She was really beginning to hate the mists.

"Cat-Man?" It was Amber questioning this time, though she sounded at least intrigued rather than like she was looking down on anyone.

"A cat-sìth who was travelling with us. His sister died saving Izban."

"What?" the beithir demanded, her green eyes almost glowing in the dim light. "Izban nearly died?" Amber's tail swished back and forth violently.

Macey wanted to remind her to calm down, and that if she wasn't careful, her tail would break something. But the last thing she wanted was for the beithir to shift completely and end up destroying the whole pub.

"You have three men?" Luch asked, drawing the attention of the other three women.

She was leaning back over a chair, an amused smile on her face.

"Yes," Macey answered simply.

"Sounds fun," Luch responded. "But Amber, your man isn't dead. He was just in danger. And I should point out, we're all currently in danger anyway. It's not like you didn't nearly die a couple of times yourself."

Amber deflated, the mouse's words sinking in and making sense to her.

"I suppose." She pouted, clearly not happy.

"Izban was fine when I saw him, which was after the cu-sìth died," Macey said, hoping it offered some comfort to the other woman.

"That was months ago though."

"I know." Macey sighed. "I'm worried about them too."

"Nothing bad can have happened to them, right?" She sounded on the edge of tears. Not that Macey could blame her given the earlier sobs.

"I don't know," she admitted honestly. Maybe that wasn't the best choice this time, but she couldn't bring herself to lie.

"Sweetheart, why are hanging out with three men?" Aunt Nessie picked up the earlier thread of conversation again, making Macey increasingly uncomfortable. Her aunt using modern language like 'hanging out' was never a good sign.

"Have you ever heard of the prophecy of the Wardens?" she asked tentatively and her aunt nodded.

"Of course, hasn't everybody?"

"So, you know how there are seven Wardens who have to save the world... well, it turns out that I'm one of them. Amber is another."

Nessie looked at her in excitement.

"Are you sure?"

"I have the marks to prove it."

"How many do you have, Macey?" Aunt Nessie asked, breaking through the emotion.

"Four. Earth, Fire, Wind and Lightning," she replied instantly, listing them in her head. She still found it odd she didn't have her own mark but figured that might just come last.

"And you definitely still have them all?"

Macey looked at Amber, who'd checked out her back earlier to describe what the new one looked like.

"Yes, they're all there," she replied in Macey's stead.

"And you've never had the other three?"

Macey shook her head.

"Then I think it's safe to say the four people whose marks you bear are safe. I do believe they'd fade if the person died."

Panic began to fill Macey at the thought. She hated the idea of any of them in danger and knowing that their marks would fade too was almost too much.

"But that means they're okay?" she asked hastily.

"I believe so. Though I can't speak for Ice or Air. I'm assuming you're Water?" Aunt Nessie leaned back, lost in thought.

"The guys seemed to think so, yes."

"Have you considered that you might not be?" Aunt Nessie asked, leaving everyone in stunned silence.

"Well, what else would I be?" Macey asked slowly. "I know for sure that Izban is ice, and I very much doubt I'm Air."

"Amber, dear," Nessie suddenly turned to the beithir. "Do you have any marks?"

The young woman shook her head. "No, but then, Izban and I haven't... we only just met."

"Wait, how did Macey get your mark then? Are you into women?" Nessie's eyes widened.

Macey snorted. "I didn't sleep with Amber. She tried to kill me."

Nessie seemed confused. "Why would she do that?"

"Long story. The same person who was holding me prisoner forced her to attack me. It wasn't her fault, really."

"But it gave you a mark?" Nessie asked, still frowning.

"Yes, it did. Amber says it's the same size as that of my men... I mean the other Wardens. It's as if there's no difference between her bond to me and theirs."

"Except that I don't want to jump you," Amber laughed. Suddenly, Macey regretted telling her about what she and the guys had been up to. It was a bit embarrassing now, come to think of it.

"No, I'm glad you don't. Three people are definitely enough for me."

Aunt Nessie tsked. "I don't know how you do it, girl. Your uncle was unbearable most of the time, and imagining three of him... no thanks."

Macey had never met her uncle, he had died before she was even born. A fishing accident involving a sharp hook and an ignorant human.

Nessie had been on her own for a long time, and secretly, Macey was sure that she enjoyed it. She could hang out with the local fishermen all day, have some fun with tourists and spend her money on whatever she wanted. Not that she hadn't done that when her husband was still alive, but at least now, there was nobody to explain herself to when she bought yet another Nessie plush animal. Her whole house was full of them; she loved the irony of Nessie buying tacky Nessies.

"Anyway, why would you doubt that I'm Water?"

"Repeat the prophecy for me, dearie," Nessie asked and Macey did as she asked. She knew it by heart by now, anyway.

"Fire and Wind,

brothers in arms,

lost in the mist.

Earth will join,

Always hungry,

Only sated by meeting the fourth.

Water will run, circling Fire,

then Wind and Earth.

Lightning is trapped,

Ice will break the chains.

Finally, Air is waiting,

only to appear

when the end is near."

Nessie ran a hand through her white hair. "I assume Fire and Wind are two of your men?"

Macey nodded. "Yes, and Earth. That's Jared. And I'm sure about all of their elements. Amber is Lightning, again, no doubt about that, and Izban is Ice. Leaves Water and Air. And it says Air won't appear until the end, but I've been here all along. No, I'm sure I'm Water, everything else doesn't make any sense."

"Water will run, circling Fire, then Wind and Earth," Nessie repeated. "Have you circled them?"

Macey blushed. In a way, she guessed she had. She'd claimed them as hers; they were her three men.

"I suppose so."

"Then you must be Water," Aunt Nessie said emphatically.

Luch chuckled. "Didn't she say that from the beginning? Why all the doubting?"

Nessie shot an angry look at the mouse. "I had a thought, a theory, but it seems I was mistaken. But I'm sure my niece is grateful to have talked through it all."

Macey hastened to nod in agreement. It was always good to be on her aunt's side. And as she still didn't know who or what Luch was, it was doubly good.

Then she remembered that there was a second prophecy that Amber didn't know about yet.

"When the cu-sìth died, she said something that sounded like yet another prophecy."

Nessie took a large sip from the ale the bartender had brought her a while ago. "Go on."

Macey tried remembering. She wasn't as sure about the exact wording as she had been about the other one.

"For my last act upon this earth,
Before I head to my rebirth,
I bequeath upon to thee,
A name which comes in three.
Macey must be the first,
Reveal the second and be cursed,
The third you shall obtain,
When Seven Wardens shall reign."

She shrugged. "Any idea what that could mean?"

Nessie whispered the words again, and Amber looked like she was repeating them in her head. Luch was the only one who seemed bored. She was staring at the pint of ale longingly, but Macey wasn't about to give beer to a mouse.

"That's all very mysterious," the beithir finally said. "Should we even be talking about that one? We don't want to accidentally reveal the second name and be cursed. Whatever that means."

"Why did you come to me?" Nessie suddenly asked.

Macey shrugged, giving her aunt a smile. "You always know an answer to everything. You're old, you've seen a lot."

Nessie's hair took on a green glow. "Did you just call me old?!" she thundered, but there was a twinkle in her eyes.

"You are old," Luch confirmed. When Nessie looked at the mouse, the twinkle disappeared.

"And you're even older, so be quiet."

Amber cleared her throat uncomfortably. "How do you two know each other?"

"We've crossed paths once or twice before," Luch said with a grimace that spoke of her distaste for the kelpie. When she stayed quiet and all Nessie did was glare at her, it was clear neither of the two was going to expand on that. Macey made a mental note to ask one of them in private at some point in the future. Or preferably both; it sounded like a tale best heard from both perspectives.

"I'm flattered that you think I know everything, dearie, but I'm afraid this time, I'm not quite sure what to tell you," Nessie finally said, ignoring the previous exchange with Luch. "I don't know what's wrong with the world or why we currently need Wardens to fix it. I believe the last time the Wardens appeared, there was a clear reason. This time, it's not as simple."

"So far, all we've found out is that the Staran is ill," Macey explained. "Malan said nobody is attacking it and that it isn't hurting itself, so there must be another reason for it. But so far, we've not really found an answer. Unless my men discovered something while I was held prisoner."

Suddenly, a strange feeling came over her. A longing, a tugging. Something deep inside of her. Then, voices appeared in the quiet pub, very familiar voices. She jumped up and ran towards the bar, where her three guys were standing.

Finally, she had them back. She was never going to let them go again.

6

S he collapsed into Flint's arms, feeling both Jared and Cam reaching out to touch her. The warmth was welcome. As was the press of their firm bodies against hers.

Another sob escaped her. But this time, she didn't hold back, and the tears began to flow. While it hadn't felt like a couple of months during her time with the Voice, it sure felt like that now.

"Hey, no crying, we're here." Flint smoothed her hair back as he whispered the words to her. But it didn't help.

"Let's get her back in here," Cam said, and she imagined him gesturing back towards the hall she'd just left. That was probably a good idea. Then again, her waiting for them to get in there also would have been. But going on another moment without them just wasn't an option.

"Here, let me." Jared scooped her up in his arms, pulling her away from Flint. She let him do it, despite not liking that she was only touching one of them. She just hoped the other two would make contact again once they were back inside the room and comfortable again.

Macey snuggled into Jared's chest, the smooth and easy rhythm of his heart soothing her in a way she hadn't expected.

"It's good to have you back in my arms, little kelpie. I've been feeling your absence."

Her eyes shot open, and she sniffed loudly. "You've been suffering? I'm sorry." She lifted a hand and pressed it against his cheek.

Jared smiled down at her while he walked. "A little, but not as much as before I met you. The others suffered too."

"I know. But you..."

"Macey, it's okay. We managed, and we found you. Or you found us..."

"Or Fedelm found all of us?" she suggested with a weak smile.

"Yes, thank goodness for interfering ghosts." Jared's smile widened, and she felt him relax. "You look thin."

"I've been a captive for two months, what do you

expect?" she answered instantly, almost demanding he set her down so she could prove just how fine she was. But she refrained. Realistically, she didn't want to leave his arms, or his touch. She'd missed them all far too much for that.

"I'm sorry."

"For what?" She cocked her head to the side, but even this close together, he managed to avoid her gaze. "You're not to blame for me being caught. No more than Izban's to blame for Amber's capture," she told him, thinking back to the beithir's story. From what she'd said, there was almost no way Amber could have avoided being caught, so she assumed the same was true for her.

"We should have been more careful though. If we'd taught you to strengthen your mental walls more, then maybe none of this would have happened..."

"And maybe it would have just happened a different way," she replied softly. "Whatever the cause, the outcome is the same. But we're here, we're safe now, and we're now only one Warden short. I'd say that's pretty good going really. Despite it all, we're further forward than we were." As she spoke, the words embedded themselves in her mind too. It was true. Despite it all, they'd come out of it with more allies, and more Wardens. Everything was further forward than it had been.

"I suppose, but we lost two months with you." Jared's voice cracked, and she began to understand the true problem. It wasn't that their mission had been side tracked. It was that they'd missed her.

"What's two months when we have forever." She turned his face towards her so he had to look her in the eyes.

"I hate to break it to you, but we're long lived, not immortal."

She laughed, the tears finally clearing. But it was a relief, especially with amusement in Jared's eyes. He was relaxing already. Being back with them was a relief.

"An incubus, Macey? I'm impressed." Aunt Nessie's laugh boomed through the room, gaining everyone's attention.

Macey wiggled slightly, and Jared listened, setting her down on the floor so she could stand on her own two feet.

"Auntie, this is Jared, Flint and Cam." She gestured to each of them as she introduced them. "This is my Aunt Nessie," she added, perhaps needlessly. None of her men had confused expressions on their faces.

"Meaning you must be Izban," Nessie addressed the blue-haired mage, who was hanging about and trying not to look at Amber.

Macey rolled her eyes. Were the two of them seriously going to ignore whatever it was between them and just dance around one another?

"Hi," Amber squeaked, stroking her tail in a move that reminded Macey of when she wrung her own hands. It was nervousness all over.

"Hello," Izban replied.

"I'm sorry," they both blurted at the same time, before going back to their shy nervousness.

"Should I mention the sexual tension I can feel emanating from them?" Jared whispered in Macey's ear, causing her to giggle.

"Behave."

"With you around? Never."

She smiled wider than she had in days, glad to be back in their comforting presence.

"There's a quiet room just off to the left," Fedelm piped up. "If you want to use it," she added hastily, probably sensing the tension in the air.

"Thanks," Amber said. "Izban, do you want to talk?" She didn't look like the same confident woman Macey had come to know already. She hoped she didn't come across quite the same when she was around her men. The last thing she wanted was to come across as useless when she was with her partners.

"Sure." He seemed just as nervous as she was, for which Macey was glad. Even if it did put his personality completely at odds with everything she'd come to know about him already. Gone was his snark and sarcasm. Even his eyes had softened. Amber was definitely his soft spot then.

She supposed she was Flint, Cam and Jared's soft spot too, so she couldn't blame the Ice Warden.

Amber and Izban disappeared into the other room, and Macey hoped they'd talk about their feelings for each other. Even she could feel the sexual tension between them, and she wasn't an incubus like Jared.

"If I was polite, I'd leave too, but I'm not," Aunt Nessie cackled. "Sit down, boys, and let me find out if you're good enough for my favourite niece."

Macey cringed. This was going to be terrible. Nessie was not known for someone who minced her words. And even though she was not the monster everyone thought her to be, she could have a nasty verbal bite.

Luch was rubbing her tiny hands in anticipation of the coming interrogation. That's what it was going to be, Macey was sure of it. Her aunt was going to make sure they were worthy of her niece.

They all sat down around the table and Nessie waved to the bartender to get them some drinks. Five glasses of ale arrived a moment later; it was as if the landlord had already prepared them in advance.

"Now tell me, boys, who of you is the strongest?" Aunt Nessie grinned widely, while Macey wanted to sink into the ground. Luckily, her men were taking it in their stride.

"I usually win in arm wrestling," Cam said cheerily, knowing exactly what he was evading the older kelpie's question. "But we're all pretty well matched."

Nessie smiled patiently. "And what are your weaknesses?"

"Water." Flint cringed, but then hurried to add, "Not Macey, though."

Jared chuckled. "I'm an incubus, I think you can imagine what my greatest weakness is."

Cam was frowning, obviously trying to come up with a good answer. "Boredom," he said eventually. "It's like a windless place, no movement, no energy."

"Good answers," Nessie admitted. "But if you're all so strong and wise, why didn't you rescue my niece?" Her expression turned serious. "Why did she have to escape herself rather than be freed by the three of you?"

"Auntie, I'm not a damsel in distress," Macey protested. "I didn't need rescuing."

Nessie looked at her with a piercing glance. "Can you honestly tell me that your imprisonment did not hurt you? That it would have been less painful if you'd been rescued earlier?"

Macey averted her gaze, unable to lie to her aunt. She was right. It had been a terrible experience. She could feel the scars inside of her, waiting to burst open in a quiet moment. She was going to have to work through all that happened. But not now. She had work to do. They all had. She just hoped that Amber could leave the past few months behind as well. The beithir had been in captivity for far longer than she had, and she was surprised at how well Amber was taking it all. Too well, almost. The big crash was going to be terrible, if it happened.

"We were searching for her," Cam said quietly. "But Izban's tracking spell didn't work, so we had nothing to go on. We tried all sorts of things. Izban stayed behind to research spells, but the three of us travelled on the Staran, asking them to bring us to Macey. They never did. So, we asked around."

"We went back to the fir na ghorma," Flint continues their story. "And to Malan, of course, and even to the sìth. But they were hesitant to talk to us, being men and all."

"Wait, what?" Macey asked in confusion. She didn't quite see the logic behind that statement.

"The sìth are matriarchal," Jared explained. "Their women are the ones in power, and men are commodities at best. So, three men wandering into their queendom to ask for help didn't go down well. They did make a few comments about the Staran though, as if they know something. We should definitely go there again, but this time, with you and Amber. They're more likely to talk to you."

"Sounds like a plan," Macey agreed, glad that they had a new lead. If the Staran were no longer letting people travel as before, time was running out for all of them. They needed to find a solution, fast.

"I hate saying this, but you should also talk to the selkies," Nessie said with a grimace. "I've heard rumours that they've started coming on land more and more because they're having trouble at sea. Maybe that's something to do with the same mess you're trying to fix."

Macey shuddered. She really didn't feel like talking to a selkie, or several at that. She'd never met one in person, but with all she'd heard about them, she didn't want to. They were the ones spreading bad rumours about kelpies, and after meeting Mhara, it seemed the same was true for the ceasg.

All in all, visiting the sìth sounded a lot better than going to the selkies. Macey knew it wasn't very grown up to do the easy option first, but she felt like she deserved it after being imprisoned by the Voice. The universe had a lot to make up for.

"I've been wondering," Nessie suddenly said. "When you take your men to bed, do you take all of them at the same time?"

"Auntie!" Macey called out, mortified. "That's none of your business."

The old kelpie chuckled. "Indulge me, darling."

"No way."

Luckily, Amber and Izban chose that moment to come back, walking hand in hand. Macey smiled in relief. It looked as if they'd had a proper chat. And judging from Amber's red lips, they maybe did even more than just talk.

Good. Now they had a couple and a quad in their Wardens relationship. Where did the seventh Warden fit in though? Macey didn't really feel like adding another person to her strange harem. Three men were enough work. She knew that they were all aching to spend some time with her, and so was she. Not just all three of them together, but some one-on-one time with each of them. But there was likely not going to be a chance for it in quite a while.

They had a world to save.

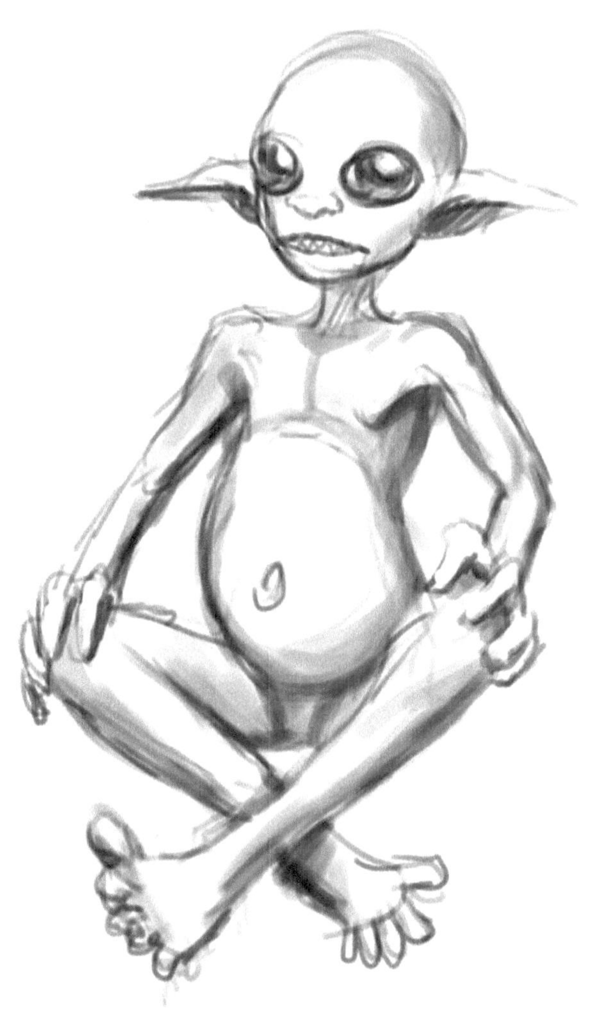

Aos Sìth

7

Leaving her Aunt was hard. There was something about her that made Macey feel safe and secure. Probably just the blood connection. And she was missing it already.

On the other hand, not having her Aunt about did mean that the awkward questions wouldn't happen anymore.

Hopefully.

Even so, telling Luch and Amber about her love life seemed far less weird than telling her Aunt. More like telling friends, even if she wasn't sure if that's what Luch was.

The seven of them were expelled from the Staran with a great thump, resulting in Macey sprawled on top of Jared. Not the worst place to be, but she'd much rather they be up to something different.

"Well, hello there." He waggled his eyebrows at her, and she smiled suggestively in return, before winking at him.

Now wasn't going to be the time for anything fun like that, but she didn't want him thinking she'd lost interest in the past few months. Maybe her men would get the wrong idea the first time they saw her new mark. She mused over whether it would be fun to let them think she and Amber had been up to a lot more than pretending to kill each other when she got it or not. It would certainly be interesting to discover how they felt about it. There was no telling whether they'd come down on the side of it being hot, or if their jealousy would get the better of them.

Not that it mattered anyway. She wouldn't do anything with Amber even if they didn't have their own men each. The beithir wasn't really her type.

From the way she was giggling and leaning into Izban, he was hers though. Even her tail was getting in on the action, as she'd curled it around his waist.

Macey frowned and cocked her head to the side, briefly wondering what it'd be like to have a tail while in human form. Weird and annoying, was her guess. But Amber didn't seem bothered by it. And it actually kind of suited her. An evolutionary trait of beithirs no doubt.

"Are we in the right place?" Macey asked Cam as she got to her feet. She wasn't sure when he'd become their resident compass, but he always seemed to fill that role.

"We sure are." He swallowed nervously, looking up at the slightly imposing building before them.

"It glitters," Macey blurted.

"Yes," Cam replied. "But don't be fooled. Not everything in the queendom is what you expect. The sìth are master magic wielders, and conjuring is their pleasure. What looks like one thing, may in fact be something very, very different. Be prepared for that."

"Sounds ominous." Macey considered back through all the stories she'd heard about the sìth, which admittedly, wasn't many. She'd learned more of the different races since meeting her men than she had before that. And if her men said to be wary, and that not everything should be taken at face value, then she was going to listen.

"Izban, if you'll do the honours," Flint instructed.

The blue-haired mage unentwined himself with Amber and held out his palm flat. He twisted what looked like a wooden ring, and after a moment, a small blue creature appeared.

Macey let out a squeak of surprise. She really should be used to the weird things that happened when she was around her men. This entire adventure had been a crazy ride. And yet, things just kept taking her off guard.

"Is that a baby Gollum?" she asked in confusion

but Izban ignored her.

The blue creature made a series of chirping noises, leaving everyone but Izban looking a bit bewildered.

"Yes, I know you haven't had long to recover. I'm sorry about that, but we're at the sìth queendom now, I'll find you a great offering," he said with a sigh.

The creature chirped again.

"Yes, the others will find you an offering too."

"Hold on a minute," Luch butted in for the first time. "You're not making me beholden to an aos sìth."

The tiny blue fairy put its arms on its hips and glared at Luch. It was about the same size as the mouse shifter, who was riding in Macey's shirt once again. It looked humanoid, except that it was blue, had long pointy ears and limbs that looked a little too large for its body. And right now, it was very, very annoyed.

"Fine, I'll find you something," Luch gave in when the aos sìth began to shout angrily. "Now, can someone explain how that blue-haired mage got himself one of the Folk?"

Izban shrugged. "I inherited him, he's been with my family for a long time. I gave him the chance to leave when I got him, but he decided to stay. He comes in handy, and all I have to give him to make him happy is milk and bread."

The aos sìth turned to Izban and swung his tiny fist while continuing to chirp.

"He wants me to tell you that he's also the main source of my magic," Izban translated. "And that I'm honoured to have him. And that I can be a right bast... No, stop it."

Amber laughed brightly and Macey smiled at seeing the beithir so cheery. This was the first true laugh she'd heard from her. Hopefully, everything was going to be okay with her and Izban.

"You don't have your own magic?" Macey blurted out, instantly regretting it. That had been rude of her.

"I do," Izban replied calmly, in a way that suggested it wasn't the first time he'd had to answer that question. "But it's limited to certain things. For others, I rely on my aos sìth. It's the same for other mages too."

"And is he the reason your hair is..." she trailed off, not believing how rude she was being. This wasn't the diplomacy she'd been brought up to exhibit.

Izban just laughed. "No, he's nothing to do with my hair. That was one of my cousins when we were younger. She got a little carried away, and it's been blue ever since. I tried to dye it once, but trust me, it's not something you want me to ever repeat again."

Macey smiled at the mage, noting he was already more relaxed than he had been. And far less aggressive. Even less so than when the Voice had given her and Amber the horrible vision.

The aos sìth's head had been turning back and forth as they spoke, but now, he looked towards the palace in front of them.

"Go," Izban commanded.

The little blue creature gave him a look that Macey could only describe as sassy, before leaping into the air, and floating off towards the drawbridge.

"Why do we need to send him?" Macey asked.

"The sìth tend to be a little more receptive if it's one of their own kind knocking on the door. With Cat-Man still missing, the aos sìth is pretty much what we have," Cam explained.

"What happened to Cat-Man?" Macey asked. She hadn't really expected the cat-sìth to still be with her men, but she was still sad not to see him. They'd become friends of a fashion, at least, she wanted to think so. His sister did make a prophecy about her after all.

"We're not sure. When we left the warehouse, he was gone. I think he'll be back if you ever need him," Cam replied.

"You do?" She frowned, not sure where the thoughts were coming from.

"Yes. You made an impression on him, whether he wanted to admit it or not. I don't think he'll show up for just anything, but if you need him, he'll be there."

"I hope you're right," Macey answered, a sense of dread filling her. She wasn't sure how this was all going to end. But she hadn't ruled out some kind of battle. Against what, she wasn't sure. But the Voice could control people, it wasn't inconceivable that he would take over the minds of an army.

Which would leave them completely screwed. Seven Wardens standing against an army of warriors with no minds of their own. It didn't sound like a very even match to her. Or to anyone.

She was pulled from her thoughts by the loud clanking of the drawbridge lowering. Everyone's attention was drawn that way. The aos sìth chirped again as it landed back on Izban's hand, before disappearing as quickly as it came.

"We're going to have to find some really good bread and milk before he'll do anything for us again," Izban muttered.

"What counts as really good?" Amber asked, leaning on his shoulder.

"Some kind of fancy sweetened bread, I'd guess? I'm not really sure, he's never told me what he likes and what he doesn't."

"Typical man then," the beithir teased.

Macey laughed as the men began to mumble.

"Oh shh, let's just get going," she ordered them.

"Do we have a plan?" Amber asked softly.

"I think it's basically, they say nothing, us three do

all the talking." Macey shrugged. That was in line with everything they'd said so far.

"Oh no, not me. I'm waiting here for you all." Luch shook her head wildly and took a step back. "No chance. No."

"Are you okay?" Amber asked, her brow creasing.

"I'm not going anywhere near any sìth."

"You were just near one," Amber pointed out, nodding in Izban's direction.

"That's different. I'm not going into a sìth palace. Trust me, it'll hurt your cause."

Macey frowned at the mouse, trying to make sense of what she was saying.

"But you'll be here when we come back out?" she asked, hating the idea of having another ally just vanishing after they went in somewhere.

"Yes. You're not done with me yet," Luch replied. "There's far more to our story together."

Macey didn't comment. She didn't really know how. The wording was odd to say the least, and made it sound a little ominous. There was very little doubt that Luch was more than just the mouse she claimed to be.

"Alright then, we go in there, and Amber and I take the lead. Luch stays behind," she changed the plan.

"I'll stay with her," Jared put in. "That way you'll know for sure she'll still be here."

Luch made an odd huffing sound. "I'm hardly going to run off, incubus. And if you think you could keep me here if I didn't want to be, then you have another thing coming."

"I'm sure you could give anyone the slip," Jared responded. "But realistically, it's safer for us all if we're not split up too much."

"That is true. Though I don't think Mahoun can touch me." The mouse seemed confident about that, and Macey supposed she should be. There was no telling how long she'd lived in the Voice's fortress, but it was long enough to have known Amber the whole time she was imprisoned, and to have a good knowledge of the whole place.

"Will you be okay?" Macey asked Jared, turning to face him. She didn't like the idea of leaving him behind, but the logic was sound. She didn't want Luch escaping until she had some answers from the woman.

Mostly about what she really was, because a mouse shifter certainly wasn't the answer. Not with how at odds she'd been with Aunt Nessie. Or how knowledgeable she'd seemed with Fedelm. If Macey had been a younger, and less worldly, kelpie, she'd have thought Luch was one of the gods she knew didn't really exist. In some ways, it was the only explanation.

"Yes," he said, stepping towards her. He cupped

Macey's cheek in his hand and lifted her face so she was looking up at him. "I'll always be okay so long as I know you're safe."

Jared leaned down and captured her lips with his, giving her the sweetest kiss she'd ever received from her incubus. He wasn't normally this restrained. Her captivity really must have been hard on him.

"Alright, you two, time to get going," Flint said, breaking Jared and Macey apart.

"Just because you want some time with her," Jared teased.

"You're damn right, I do. But maybe not when we're waiting outside the sìth's home. I'd rather not be at their mercy any longer than necessary."

"Flint's right," Izban added. "For the same reasons you don't want to go in there." He smirked at Jared.

"Wait, what's going on? Why don't you want to go in there?" Macey demanded of her incubus.

"The sìth view men as playthings if you will. And we're no exception," Cam answered instead, exchanging a quick glance with Flint.

"They also like to share," Luch piped up, drawing dirty look from the two men. The mouse shrugged. "It's true. They'll see Macey and Amber as having surplus men, and therefore, those men are fair game. And an incubus... well, there's not a woman on earth who wouldn't want one of those in her bed."

Macey growled, a sound she was pretty sure she'd

never made before. But no one was even going to suggest touching any of her men.

"I didn't say I'd do anything about it," Luch added hastily, holding up her hands in surrender. "But doesn't mean I'm not thinking it."

"Find your own," Macey snapped.

"Oh, I just might. You've given me some rather interesting ideas, kelpie." The mouse sounded almost too happy, but Macey didn't wait for clarification.

"Erm..."

"Just where did you find them? I should go there to look for myself," Luch mused.

"They found me," Macey said, bewildered by the turn of the conversation.

"Oh, what a pity. Guess I'll just have to find myself some men elsewhere."

"I don't know how you'd cope," Amber muttered, looking at Izban under her lashes.

Macey smothered a laugh. The beithir had made it pretty clear that she didn't want more than just Izban. Macey found it sweet, but couldn't help but compare it to how she'd felt before meeting her men. There'd been no thoughts of having more than one of them from here either. Not even in her wildest imagination.

"Problems for another day, you'd better get going, the sìth will be expecting you."

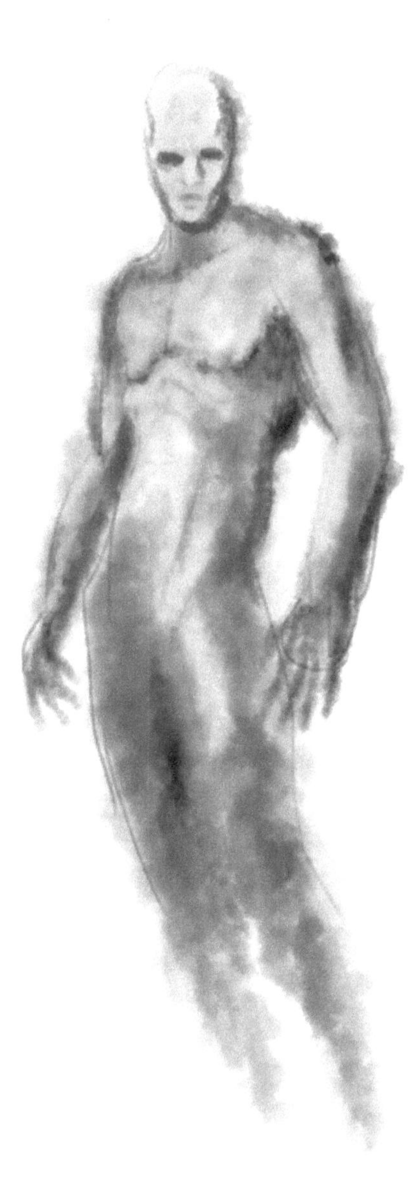

Seelie

8

Beyond the drawbridge and the gate, a beautiful sight awaited the Wardens. Macey had a hard time not walking around with an open mouth, gaping at the scene presenting itself. She'd expected buildings made from the same glittering material as the outside walls. Instead, she was walking on clouds. It wasn't the mist of the Staran, no, it was thick, white clouds that were covering the ground - or maybe they were the ground? It was the same with all the buildings that reached far into the distance: they were made of clouds, their walls white and uneven and looking incredibly soft. Macey was tempted to touch one of the walls to see if she could walk through it. But after what she'd heard of the sìth, she didn't want to make a bad impression on them. This was the time to show some diplomacy.

They carefully walked further into the wide space that stretched from the gate they'd come through to a large, tall building. It didn't quite look like Macey had imagined a fairy palace, but as the biggest house of them all, it had to be the place they were going to.

No fairies were anywhere to be seen. Macey thought she could see some movements behind one of the cloudy windows of a building to her right, but maybe that was just a trick of the light. It was bright here, even though the sky was full of clouds. They weren't grey and foreboding clouds though, but friendly, white, fluffy ones. The kind of clouds children would draw.

They reached the large building, but the doors were shut. There was still nobody that seemed to be expecting them.

"Who did your little blue helper talk to?" Amber asked her almost-boyfriend and he grimaced.

"He didn't say, but I assume it was one of their guards. I'm sure they're here right now, watching us. Shall we try if the doors are open?"

Macey nodded and walked up the steps leading to the two silver doors. They were beautiful and intricately carved, showing sun rays shining down on a crowd of people who were reaching up for the sky. Were those sìth? The carvings were too small to distinguish sìth from humans. Not that Macey had ever seen a sìth, but she'd heard they had pointy ears and were a lot prettier than humans. Which didn't take much; most supernaturals were a lot more beautiful than any human would ever be.

There were no door handles, so she tried pushing the doors inwards. Nothing happened.

Looking back at her fellow Wardens for support - which they gave with a nod - she knocked on the doors as loud as she could.

The silvery metal the doors were made of was surprisingly warm against her knuckles. It definitely wasn't a material she'd find on Earth, but that really shouldn't surprise her. They were in the queendom of the sìth after all. Everything here was going to be strange and unique.

"Go away!" a high female voice called from the other side.

"I'm afraid we can't do that," Macey replied loudly. "We're here on important business that cannot wait." She was using words she'd heard her father use at court, hoping that the sìth were using a similar flowery language here.

"We're not interested in doing business with you!"

Macey sighed. "We're not trying to sell you anything. We're here to offer you our help in return for you giving us some information."

She was bluffing, of course, she didn't even know if the sìth needed any help with something. Maybe everything was fine here in the queendom. Maybe her men had misinterpreted the situation.

"What help could a kelpie, a beithir, a mage and two wraiths give us?"

Oh, so the sìth knew who they were. Or at least what they were. Did they know about Luch and Jared waiting on the other side of the gate as well?

"How about you let us in and we discuss it face to face? I'd really love to make your acquaintance."

No, she really wasn't, but a bit of flattery usually worked.

"I don't. Please leave." The woman's voice was getting ever more high-pitched and angry.

Macey sighed. "We've travelled a long way to get here. If you'd prefer to just talk to us women, the men can stay outside."

The three male Wardens huffed behind her, but she ignored them. Amber and her had proven that they could look after themselves. After all, they'd escaped the Voice without their men's help.

"I don't care if you're a woman or not. You're not welcome here, so go before I make you go."

Suddenly, the silver doors began to sizzle with electricity and Macey jumped back. She turned to Amber who had her hands outstretched, pointing towards the entrance.

"Amber, what's wrong?"

"It's my magic. They're using *my* magic. It's like

they're copying it and then using it for their own purpose. It's not draining me, but it's really uncomfortable."

When Izban heard that, he put an arm around Amber, pressing her close. She gave him a small smile, but she kept her hands outstretched as if she was trying to defend herself.

"Stop hurting my friend!" Macey shouted at the doors, anger bubbling up in her. All she'd wanted was to talk to the sìth. Weren't they supposed to be the nice ones? Or had they accidentally landed in the Unseelie Court, where the not-so-nice sìth lived?

"Shhh, over here!" someone whispered from their left. It took Macey a moment to see the woman who was pressed against the cloudy wall of the building. She almost seemed to be part of the cloud herself: her white hair blended in perfectly with her surroundings and her pale skin made an ideal camouflage. She was thin as a wisp and looked as if the slightest gust of air could blow her away. Was that a fairy?

"They won't talk to you but I know who will," the woman whispered. "Come with me."

Macey looked at the other Wardens. Was it safe to trust this sìth? Or was this a trick intended to get rid of them?

Amber shrugged. "I really want to get away from these doors, so let's see what she has to say."

Even though Amber had said that the magic wasn't draining her, her cheeks had lost a bit of colour. Yes, getting away from here sounded like a good idea.

"Let's follow her," Macey decided and ignored the doubtful looks her men were giving her. She was beginning to like the idea that the women in the queendom were in charge. Maybe it was contagious, maybe that's why she was suddenly feeling like it was best for her to make all the decisions. Of course, she'd felt like that before, but now she was actually acting on it.

With one last wistful look at the closed silver doors, she walked towards the woman who was impatiently waiting for them. Now that they were closer, it was obvious that the woman was a little older than them. Well, in looks at least. Macey was well aware that her men were older than they looked, but this woman seemed in her mid-thirties perhaps, not twenties like herself and the rest of the Wardens. Amber was the youngest at eighteen, and she didn't know how old Izban was. Maybe the same age as Macey?

But then, who cared. Age was just a number.

"Who are you?" Macey asked, but the woman just shook her head.

"Later, follow me and be quick about it."

Without further warning, she ran off, keeping close to the buildings on their right, the woman blending into the cloudy walls. Macey and the other Wardens had to stand out like dark spots on white linen. Everything here was so bright, so ethereal. It was beautiful and pure, but after her first encounter with the closed doors and the weird magic copying thing, she didn't trust the innocent looks of everything around them. Just like Cam had said, looks may be deceiving in this place.

The woman floated, which was unsurprising really, given her appearance, and was moving surprisingly quickly. Even so, the Wardens managed to keep pace, though it was growing more and more difficult. The last time Macey had slept, she'd been in captivity. The same went for Amber. The men didn't look as fresh as they could be either. It was a good job they all had the superior strength of being more than human to keep themselves going, or they'd probably be dead.

Maybe they all should be anyway. They'd been through a lot, and had several narrow escapes, none of which had left them completely whole. Mental torture took its toll too. And while Macey knew her and Amber had their own issues from the captivity to deal with, she was sure the men were suffering similarly for being away from them.

"You know, I'm kind of getting tired of blindly following people I don't know," Flint chuntered.

Macey didn't say anything. She could either agree with him, and risk turning their current host against them, or she could lie and tell him she wasn't fed up of that exact thing. Ever since she'd met her men, she'd been thrust into the position of being around people she didn't know. She was just lucky a lot of them had become her friends. More so than had become her enemies. Thankfully.

As far as she was aware, there was just the Voice who was actually against them. Though knowing her luck, there'd be someone else along the way. Not to mention, someone could betray them at any moment. Cat-man hadn't been all that friendly towards her, she reckoned he could be turned against her still.

"It's just for a little longer," Cam consoled him.

"We have a time limit?" Macey blurted, without mulling it over in her head.

She looked over her shoulder, and the guilty look on Cam's face said it all.

"I-"

"Why the fuck didn't you tell me?" she demanded.

"We didn't know until we went to see Malan again. Before that, we just thought we were going up against how sick the Staran were getting. But he..."

"How long have we got?" Amber asked, her voice soft and instantly calming the tensions rising between them all.

"About three weeks," Cam added nervously.

"Great. So, we're a Warden short, and still don't have any idea what in the waves we should be doing, and we have three measly weeks to do it? Well, didn't this month just get better." Macey turned back towards their host, watching the cloud flooring skip by.

"You might be closer than you think," the sìth in front to her said. "Sometimes answers are closer than you think," she added.

"Unless you know where the Air Warden is, and he or she has all the answers, then I very much doubt we're closer than we think," Macey replied bitterly.

"Have faith, kelpie. Have faith."

The woman pushed open one of the shiny doors, and Macey cringed inwards, hoping to avoid touching it. The last thing she wanted was it stealing her powers like it had to Amber's.

Actually, that process reminded her a little of Luch, and what the mouse had done to destroy the barrier at the ceasg's pool.

"Come in, then." The woman gestured wildly, and the Wardens hurried into the room.

The walls were made of the same swirling cloud and Macey found herself completely distracted by a pattern on the back wall. There was something about it that called to her.

"You're here," a male voice exclaimed from behind them. He sounded genuinely excited to see them. Which was both a relief, and slightly concerning.

"Hi," Macey said in return, turning around to face the man. He was pretty much exactly what she'd expected. He was like a male version of the woman who'd brought them here. Thin and wisp like.

And beautiful. Far more beautiful than anyone semi-translucent had any right to be.

"I thought sìth were supposed to have pointy ears," she muttered to herself, quietly enough so that no one else should be able to hear.

"We do, when we're in human form," the wispy man replied.

Obviously, she hadn't been speaking quiet enough. She should think before she spoke. That was what her father had always taught her, and she was honestly a little ashamed that she hadn't remembered that in the first place.

"Hello," Amber said nervously, looking at the man oddly.

"Hi," he said, offering his hand for the beithir to take. She did, and he raised her hand to his mouth and kissed it.

Amber giggled as his partly there lips brushed against her skin and Macey couldn't work out how she felt about the situation. Up until now, almost every man she'd come across had their attention on her first. Having another woman around was going to take some getting used to.

Izban, on the other hand, had his emotions written all over his face. He was jealous. Macey smothered a smile. She was sure any of her men would have had the same expression if it was her getting the sìth's attention.

At least this was more like the Izban she'd originally met, and not the man he'd apparently become in the months she'd been locked away. Of all the changes that had occurred, that was the most difficult one to fathom.

"You wanted to see us?" she asked, interrupting the moment.

Amber blushed, clashing horrendously with her hair. It must be one of the perils of being a redhead, as well as one of the reasons Macey was glad she wasn't. Clashing with her darker hair was certainly more difficult.

"Yes, I believe I have what you're looking for."

"You have a person?" Macey blurted before she could help herself.

"Sort of. What do you know about the Seelie?" he asked, drifting from side to side as he spoke.

"That they're the good guys?" Macey shrugged, not too sure what he was expecting her to say.

"I suppose in a sense. But you're not supposed to be able to see us. You only can now because we're wrapped ourselves in the clouds."

That at least made some kind of sense. They did

appear as if one wave of the hand would cut through them.

"Makes sense. But what does that have to do with the Air Warden?" she asked. Though maybe she shouldn't have admitted that was their goal so soon.

"The Air Warden isn't a person. It's something that must bond with one of you," the man said.

"You mean, share one of our bodies with another soul?" Amber interrupted, pulling a face as she did.

"No. It's not a soul, more of a power."

"That's not unheard of," Cam reasoned. "And it makes sense if it's linked to the Seelie."

"Indeed. Sometimes a voice can be heard on the wind, or a rustle in the trees, that could well be Air. But it is not a person. Just controlled by a person."

"Oh." Macey didn't know what to make of that. How were they supposed to decide who would carry the extra power? And how would it interact with the powers each of them already had?

"The question is, which one of you will it be?" the man asked, and the Wardens exchanged worried glances.

This wasn't going to be an easy choice.

9

" A re there any side effects?" Flint asked worriedly. Just like him, Macey was a little worried about this latest development. Having a seventh Warden would have been so much easier. There may have been some trouble fitting them into their current relationships - no one ever wanted to be the only one single in a group of couples... quads - but at least it would have been a living, breathing person. Macey could work with that. But having a new power... that was different.

"I'm not sure a Seelie power has ever been bound to a non-fae before," the man said softly. His voice was calming and gentle, and Macey began to wish that he'd talk to her more, about anything, everything. His voice was to die for.

"I cannot guarantee that it'll all go smoothly. But

if you want your seventh Warden, there is only that one way."

"Wait, how do you know about the Wardens?" Macey asked, suddenly suspicious despite his beautiful voice. "How do you know we're some of them?"

"The very power that is going to bind with one of you told me," the woman said, a big smile on her face. "It also told me that it's met you before, Macey. It tried to warn you once, but you didn't listen."

"What? I don't think I've ever..." A memory popped up in her head. Back at her brothers' house, when they lay unconscious outside, she'd heard a voice that told her to run. She didn't and ended up being kidnapped. Kind of. Although that was a good thing, otherwise she'd never have met her men. But wasn't there something else? She remembered how when she first woke, she'd been convinced that someone had hit her on the head. Cam had insisted that she'd fainted and she'd almost begun to believe that herself... But what if Air had warned her about whoever had attacked her, not about the kidnapping?

"So, you can talk to it?" she asked, aching for more information.

"Air talks to all of us," the man said with a grin. "We're made of the same element; you could probably call us family. Air whispers to us when humans are in need of us, and sometimes, we listen. Not as much now as we used to, but that's another story."

His smile turned sour. "There are bad things going on all over the world, and many of them are connected. Even the Seelie court has not stayed untouched by evil. But let's not speak of that. You need to make a decision. Who of you will carry Air?"

"Can we have a moment alone?" Cam asked the two sìth and with a nod, they disappeared from the room, leaving the five Wardens alone.

"We shouldn't decide this without Jared," Flint said empathically. "It's a big decision and all six of us should be involved."

"Do we have time for that?" Macey asked. "We still need to go and talk to the selkies from what Aunt Nessie said, and we only have three weeks in which to do it..."

"It'll only take half an hour or so to go talk to him," Flint pointed out.

"Will they let us back in if we leave?" Amber asked.

Macey looked at the other woman, appreciating her acuteness. That was a very good question. The sìth, or at least some of them, were co-operating at the moment, but would that continue? If they said they needed to delay, then would they still be friendly?

Sure, the Seelie Court was supposed to be the light one, but Macey doubted that was always the case. Every race had their decent folk, and their evil and twisted ones.

"I'll do it," she said suddenly, before holding up her hand. "Before you say anything, it makes the most sense. I'm the one with most of the marks already, and that's got to mean something. So, it makes sense for me to take on Air."

Macey didn't want to admit how worried that thought made her. But if it needed doing for the good of the Wardens, and the good of the world in general, then she'd do it. She needed to.

"That might be true, but..." Flint started, only to stop speaking when Cam placed a hand on his shoulder.

"It might be easiest for me to take the power. I'm Wind already, so Air would match my existing skill set."

Macey walked up to him and cupped her hand around his cheek. "Can you promise me that's the case? That it wouldn't mess with your existing magic? Or that it would be painless? Because if you can't, then you're not doing it."

"Macey..."

"Don't Macey me. There's a reason this all set in motion when I showed up. And why the marks are appearing on *my* back and not on anyone else's."

"That's not how this works," Flint protested.

"Isn't it?" She met his eyes and was floored by the

compassion and concern that lingered there. Her men certainly weren't thinking with their heads right now. They were thinking with their hearts.

"I could take it, I think," Amber piped up. "It's probably similar enough to my storm magic. But I think Macey's right, I think it needs to be her."

Macey nodded her thanks. It was good having a friend fully on her side through all this. Amber wasn't going to make decisions based on her romantic attachment to Macey, because there wasn't one. She'd logic these things out, before agreeing with whichever party made the most sense.

"I agree with Amber," Izban added.

"Of course you do. It's not your girlfriend being put in danger," Flint burst in.

"Girlfriend?" Macey raised an eyebrow at him. Now definitely wasn't the right time to be having this conversation, but she really couldn't help it. She liked the way the word sounded when he said it.

"Girlfriend doesn't even begin to sum up what you are to me," he announced.

"And do you have a word that would sum me up?" she teased.

"I don't think anything could," he answered softly, taking her hand from Cam's face, and placing it on his own. "I know a lot of things about it though. I know I love you, Macey, and I know that I couldn't live with myself if anything bad happened to you."

"I feel the same way," Macey said honestly, before looking over at Cam. "About all of you. But that doesn't mean I'm not doing this. We all know I'm the logical choice to take on Air. So that's what we're going to do."

Flint started to protest, but Macey held up her hand to stop him.

"Please, Macey," Cam tried begging.

"No. I'm doing this. I have to do this. Think about what the alternative is," she implored them, hoping that would make the difference.

"Fine."

"I'm glad to hear you've decided," the sìth man said, popping up out of nowhere and making Macey jump.

"You couldn't have knocked?" Izban demanded.

The man looked at his hands. "With what?" He seemed genuinely perplexed, and Macey had to admit he had a point. Though given his appearance out of thin air, she had some questions about why they even had doors if they weren't going to use them.

"I'm ready," Macey said. "Tell me what you want me to do."

10

The room was cold without the others in it. Though in reality, it was probably exactly the same temperature as before, the only difference was that she didn't have the protection of the other Wardens around her.

They were on the other side of the strange metal door though, so she didn't feel their absence quite as much. If Macey really wanted, she could back out of the entire thing at any point. Flint or Cam would take her place in an instant.

Which was the main reason she wasn't saying a word to them about how scared she was. If she didn't take on Air, then she might never get the mark on her back, and while she didn't know what the importance of those was, there must be one. And she didn't want to take the risk of not having the full set.

Working out how she got her own mark would be the last step, she was sure. Maybe it would happen when her own magic was completely unblocked. While the lock her father had put on her powers was almost gone, she could still feel the remnants of it holding her back.

And she hated it. She still didn't understand why he'd done that. Unless it was to teach her some humility. He'd vastly underestimated the things she'd get up to on earth if that was the case. Months imprisoned had taught her all the humility she could possibly need.

Taking a deep breath, Macey recited the words the sìth had taught her already in her head. Now wasn't the time to risk anything like getting them wrong. Not when there was so much at stake.

"Gairm èadhar airson a dhol a-steach dhomh," she said softly, hoping she'd gotten her pronunciation right.

The clouds making up the walls around her began to swirl like crazy, almost like the wind had caught them. It must be Air. After all, it couldn't be Cam. He wouldn't risk anything that could harm her.

Macey's hair whipped around her face as she was lifted off the ground by an unseen force. Breathing in and out as slowly as she could, Macey tried not to panic. She had no idea what would happen if she did.

"Do not panic, Warden." It was the same male

voice that had spoken to her before, while her brothers had been unconscious. But there was something odd about it towards the end. "I'm not going to hurt you."

This time, it was clearer. The voice wasn't male any longer. In fact, it sounded suspiciously like Macey's own voice.

"That's the idea," the voice, Air, responded. "I'm not a being in my own right. I am just part of one of the other Wardens."

Macey swallowed loudly, wondering whose voice it was Air had been mimicking before.

"The last Fire Warden," the voice said sadly. "He was the last one I joined with, so it was his voice I spoke with."

Macey nodded. That at least made some kind of sense.

"I'm going to meld with you now. But you won't hear from me again after that," Air said.

"I won't?" Macey asked, suddenly finding her voice.

"No. I'll be one with you. My powers will be yours."

"And you'll be able to use mine too?" Macey asked nervously, trying not to think about how weird it was to be having a conversation with someone that sounded just like her.

"No. I have no control at all. I'm just there."

Macey mulled it over for a moment. "So, you're about to vanish as a personality?"

"I suppose. But I didn't have a personality to begin with," Air answered.

"But you must have if you were born at some point?" Macey prodded.

"Millennia ago, maybe. But I've taken on this form for as long as I can remember. Though this is going to be the first time I've been hosted by the Water Warden. I end up with Wind or Earth more often than not."

It was slightly chilling hearing Air talk that way. Especially when Macey couldn't see the person she was conversing with. But there was very little to be done about that. She had to go ahead with this melding, or else the world was going to be more at risk than ever. Plus, it might be good to know more than Cam did for a change. So long as Air would help with her knowledge. She hoped so.

"One last thing," Macey said.

"Hmm?" Air replied.

"Do you have a name?"

Air chuckled. "You know, no one has ever asked me that."

"Indulge me," Macey replied.

"No, I don't have a name. But we, combined, do."

"Will you tell me it?" Macey asked, carefully recalling Sharara's prophetic words. If things were going as they should, then this should be her second name. The one that she couldn't reveal to anyone for risk of being cursed. That didn't sound fun.

"Yes, but you can't repeat it. Not even to your men."

"I know, if I do, I'll be cursed."

"Ah, yes, the cu-sìth's words," Air said, sounding like she'd be nodding along if she had a body.

"How do you know about that?"

"I know about most of your adventures, I've been with you almost everywhere except Mahoun's keep. I cannot go there without the body of a host."

"Makes sense," Macey muttered, trying to keep her unease at bay. Especially as Air seemed to be able to tell what she was thinking even if she didn't say it aloud.

"Sadly. But seriously, you can't say the name to anyone else."

"What will happen if I do?"

"You're looking at the consequences. Well, not looking I suppose. But you'll be cursed to an eternity of being the Seventh Warden, the one who has no body, no life of their own, and no name. As much as I long for freedom from this burden, I couldn't wish it on anyone."

"Which is why you haven't insisted when no one asked for your name," Macey mused.

"Indeed. The Wardens have a good leader with you."

"I'm not a leader," Macey protested.

"Deny it all you want, but you are. And often, the best leaders are those that don't want to be one," Air answered. "Our name is Talia. Never let it cross your lips."

"Thank you for sharing it with me," Macey said, running it around her head. It seemed to fit, in an odd way. Though it didn't make that much sense to have a name no one would know, it was hardly the strangest thing that had happened to her since she'd left the Loch.

"Thank you for talking with me, Macey. It's been a long time since anyone did that."

She wasn't sure how she knew, but those were the last words Air was going to say to her.

Macey's body returned to the floor along with a searing pain to her back. This time, she didn't panic, knowing what was there before anyone even saw it.

Five marks down, just two to go. All she had to do was persuade Izban to perform magic with her.

And then work out what she needed to do to get her own.

SOMEHOW, Macey was almost disappointed that her visit to the Seelie court had been so short. She'd heard a lot about the sìth and was curious about their lives. All she'd seen was their cloudy houses as well as the man and woman who'd told them about Air. She made a mental note to come back here, once everything was over. Of all the places she'd been recently, this was the one she found most intriguing. Visiting the storm kelpies under the sea had been fascinating, but she'd felt trapped in those big glass domes, unable to feel the water all around them. Cat-man's home had been quite boring and misty, and with his sister dead, she didn't see any reason for visiting there again. She didn't even know where the ceasg had been living, and she wasn't keen on going there again either. Although of course, her favourite place was her men's house in the mists. That strange inbetween place that changed at the whims of its inhabitants. She ached to be back there with her three lovers, spending some time with them. But they'd told her that they only had three weeks to save the world - waves, that sounded so dramatic! - so there was no time to rest and recuperate. Although they all needed to get some sleep.

"Where is Air?" Jared asked when they stepped out of the gates. Luch was sitting on the ground, licking her paws.

"Long story, but we've got our seventh Warden.

Let's go home, get some sleep and make plans for what's next," Macey said with a yawn. She'd felt a slight burst of energy when she'd joined with Air, but it wasn't enough to keep her going for much longer.

"I don't see anyone?" Jared insisted, but Cam put an arm around his friend's shoulders and quietly got him up to speed, saving Macey from having to do a long and tiring explanation. All she wanted was her bed.

"Is everyone ready to travel?" Flint asked and held out a hand. They knew the procedure by now and everybody took hold of his arm. It wasn't important to hold on tight, but there needed to be a connection to one of the two wraiths for them to travel the Staran. Both Cam and Flint had said how it was harder to enter the Staran now that they were getting even worse, but luckily, it was still possible. Macey didn't want to think about what would happen if they'd no longer be able to use them. How were they going to get from place to place? Most of the places they'd visited so far had been in other planes, not on Earth, or at least not on the Earth she'd grown up on.

Izban was the last to touch Jared's outstretched arm, but as soon as he did, they were ripped into the Staran and away from the queendom of the sìth.

THE HOUSE LOOKED JUST as welcoming as it always did. Macey was having a hard time keeping her eyes open. There was nothing but her bed on her mind. She knew she was being selfish, but she hoped her men would show Amber and Izban where to sleep. There were enough bedrooms, all they had to do was assign them one. She hoped they'd take one together and not insist on being prude.

Macey staggered to the room she was sharing with her men. She didn't even bother taking off her clothes. They'd go in the bin tomorrow anyway; they weren't much more than rags by now.

She pulled the duvet close to her chin, relishing the feeling of the soft fabric on her skin. She'd not had a proper blanket in ages, nor a mattress, nor a pillow... she fell asleep before the others could even join her.

11

Seven stone thrones in a circle. On them, six people, their backs straight, their faces serious. One of the thrones remained empty bar a strange shimmer in the air above it. And standing in the middle of the circle they formed, was Macey.

"What's going on?" she asked groggily, wiping the sleep from her eyes.

"Welcome... welcome... welcome...," it echoed through the chamber. It wasn't just one of them speaking, it was all of them in unison. Six voices, three male, three female. Together, they sounded like a Gregorian chant Macey had heard once.

Macey didn't even have to think hard to know who these people were.

"Are you the past Wardens?" she asked for clarification?

"Yes.... yes... yes... the last set."

"How many have there been?"

"Too many to count," the voices replied. "But you will be the last... the last... the last..."

The echoing was beginning to distract Macey. It was a little too dramatic for her taste.

"Why will we be last? What's so special about us?"

"You're the ones who make or break the Wardens' legacy... if you succeed, there will be no more need for us. If you fail, there will be nobody left to fight for."

Macey swallowed hard. No pressure then.

"Does that mean we'll die if we succeed?"

"No... no.... no... you'll live happily ever after."

A slight chuckle followed that last statement. Dead Wardens with a sense of humour? How very strange.

Now came the most important question. "Why am I here?"

"Do you know what to do to save the world... the world... the world?"

Macey cringed. That was the tiny problem she was trying to ignore.

"No. We know that the Staran are dying, but we don't know why or what we can do about it."

"The Staran are only one part of the whole picture. You will need to look beyond them to see the root of the evil that is spreading quickly."

"The Voice... ehm, Mahoun?"

"Again, he is only a part. There is more going on than you know, but you need to hurry up to find a solution."

Macey sighed in frustration. How did new problems keep coming along? Dealing with both the Staran and the Voice was a big enough challenge. Now they were saying that there was more? Oh waves, this was becoming an impossible mission.

"Can you help?" she asked, trying to keep desperation from sneaking into her voice.

"No... no... no..."

"Then why am I here? Just so you can tell me how hopeless everything is? How we're likely going to fail?"

"No... no... no..."

"And stop doing that echo thing!" Macey screamed, frustrated and angry. Bad news kept overwhelming here and there was no end in sight. Didn't she deserve a break? Some time with her men? A moment to recuperate from the time she'd spent as a prisoner?

One of the six people got up. His face stayed in the shadows, but it was clear that he was a man. His broad shoulders reminded her of Flint, but he looked older, even though she could just see his body.

"I'm sorry," he said calmly with a deep, gentle

voice. "We're not used to talking to outsiders. We didn't want to anger you."

"You didn't," Macey tried to backpedal. "It's just that I never seem to get good news, it's always doom and gloom. And with every answer we find, ten more questions pop up. It's so frustrating."

The man chuckled softly. "I remember that feeling. It seems not much has changed for the next generation of Wardens. But don't despair, there is always hope. As long as the seven of you are together, there is still a chance to fulfil your purpose."

"I don't have all the marks yet," Macey admitted.

"You will have them, soon. But you won't need them until the very end, so don't worry."

"So they're important?"

The man laughed again. "Oh yes, they're very important. Right now, though, you should focus on something else. The Staran won't let you travel on them for much longer. You need to stabilise them before you can proceed to deal with the other issues. A certain mouse should be able to help you."

"Luch? But she's not said anything about the Staran so far?"

"She? Is she pretending to be a woman this time?"

Macey nodded, remembering how surprised she was when Luch had first appeared in her human form. As a mouse, she didn't have a defined gender, but if Macey'd had to choose back then, she'd said it was a male mouse.

"Luch shows itself as whatever it wants to be. It must be in a feminine mood at the moment, or maybe it didn't want to look like competition to your husbands."

"Wait, they're not my husbands," Macey interrupted. "We're not married. I only met them... well, not long ago."

"Oh, I'm sorry, sometimes it's hard to keep the present and future apart." The man cleared his throat uncomfortably. "Although we see many futures, and only one of them will come to pass."

"So, you can see a future where I'm married to my men?" Macey asked, wide-eyed.

"Yes, in several of them. The ones in which you win."

Macey smiled grimly. "How do I win? Who do I need to fight?"

"That will very much depend on the path you choose to take," the man answered.

"Helpful," Macey muttered. Even though this was a dream, and there'd be no way of hiding her thoughts and feelings.

"I know. I remember being in your position. Nothing seems to help, and everything seems to get more complicated by the minute."

"You can say that again," Macey said darkly.

"Though I'll admit, I only had one man to deal with, rather than three." The man chuckled to himself. "You really did make things that bit more complicated for yourself."

"They're the least complicated bit," she protested. "With them I know where I stand. They love me, I love them," she admitted, before realising it was the first time she'd ever said it out loud. She'd tell them about it later though. Right in the middle of the most stressful situation of their entire lives.

"I'm glad to hear it. I remember that feeling too." He glanced over his shoulder, and back towards where the other past Wardens were seated.

"Is this place we're in somewhere us Wardens need to go?" Macey asked.

"No. This isn't really a place as such. More an echo of what is past. The thrones do exist. But they existed where we needed them to and will exist where and when you need them too."

"So, they'll just appear?" That should have surprised her. Or freaked her out. Or something, but it'd had gotten to the point where nothing was surprising her.

"I assume so. They did for us."

"But aren't you just human?" she blurted out, remembering something Malan had said.

"Yes. And I believe that's where the world has been going wrong. With the exception of Air, all any of us have ever been is human. It came as even more of a shock to us than it did to you."

"I must admit, finding shifters along the way hasn't been the weird bit."

"Exactly." The man looked off into the distance. "The road ahead is tough, Macey. You need to be prepared."

"Can you help me?" she asked hopefully.

"No, I don't believe so. The trials you have to face are too shrouded in mystery for anyone to see. Even prophets such as Malan and Fedelm will struggle to see your true path. There are so many you could take. In some, your battle is internal. A battle for yourself so to speak. In others, the war encompasses all manner of beings. And the people you've befriended along the way, are those that will aid you here."

"So, what you're saying is that anything could happen to me?"

"Pretty much." The man shrugged. "But I suspect the truth lies somewhere between there. You will have mental battles to face. Mahoun is trying to stop the prophecy coming to pass, though what's in it for him, is beyond anything I know. On paper, he has nothing to gain from the Staran dying. Nor from the things that would die after that."

"Because there's far more at risk than just our way of travelling?" she clarified.

"The whole world is at risk. Everything. Each

type of magical being, every way of life. Even the humans are in danger."

"Got it. If I fail, everything will die. The world will implode. Nowhere will be left untouched."

"Pretty much, yes."

"Cheery thought."

"It's rather a heavy weight to bear. Our Wind Warden almost lost her mind over the pressure. I can empathise. She was only fifteen at the time. It's a lot to take in at that age," he said wistfully.

"At any age," Macey returned. "I don't think this would be any easier if I was as old as Aunt Nessie."

"Ah, yes, Nessie. She was only young when I met her, but she made an impression on Jonas."

"Jonas?" Macey echoed. "That was aunt's first husband's name"

"You don't know?" The man seemed surprised.

"Obviously not, please enlighten me."

"This place both exists, and does not," he started. "People can visit if they so wish."

"Go on..." Macey prompted, a sinking feeling she knew where this was going.

"We were the Wardens a hundred or so years ago, when your Aunt was a young kelpie, just exploring the world. Not unlike you, actually."

"Please tell me you're not saying what I think you are?" Macey shook her head from side to side, trying to rid herself of the images that had taken root there.

"Jonas and Nessie fell for each other instantly. Almost like it was written in the stars so to speak. They were inseparable until it came time for the final battle."

He looked away, sadness etched all over his face.

"They're lucky they still found a way to be able to meet. She used to come here once a week or so. Until about twenty-two years ago. She stopped then. We haven't seen her since."

He looked back towards the other Wardens.

"Which Warden was Jonas?" Macey asked, pretty sure she already knew the answer. There was only one way this was going, and she wasn't sure what to make about it.

"Water, but I think you already knew that." He smiled weakly.

"It makes sense. Kelpies are drawn to water."

"And to Wind, Fire and Earth apparently." He smiled coyly and Macey laughed.

"Apparently so."

"Jonas is a good man. Though he's fading now. We all are, to make way for you."

"I'm sure he is. I'd never think my ex-Uncle was anything else." And it did explain why her Aunt had always seemed so distant from the uncle Macey could remember."

"He's not your ex-uncle, Macey. He's your father."

12

With a gasp, Macey woke up.

"What's wrong?" Jared asked sleepily and pushed himself up until he was looking straight at her. "Bad dream?"

"You could say that," Macey muttered, still trying to get her head around what'd just happened. It didn't feel like a dream. The image of the room with the stone thrones and her conversation with one of the previous Wardens was as clear a memory. It had to be a memory. It was real.

Which meant that everything she knew about her family was a lie.

"I need to see Nessie," she announced and got up, struggling with the blanket which had tangled itself around her legs. No, that wasn't a blanket. That was Flint, stretched out diagonally over the bed.

"Huh?" He rubbed his eyes and looked at her in confusion. "Why are you kicking me?"

"I thought you were the duvet," Macey mumbled. "Now get off my legs, I need to kill a certain loch monster."

Cam cleared his throat. "Ehm, I'm sorry to be a spoilsport but you may want to put some clothes on first."

A moment later, Macey was back under the covers, hiding her naked body. Not from the guys. From herself. The universe.

"What would you do if you suddenly found out that your parents aren't your real parents?" she asked, her voice close to a whisper.

"Burn someone?" Flint suggested.

"Did you have a bad dream?" Cam asked, making Macey glare at him furiously.

"Don't patronise me! It wasn't a dream, it was real. I met Wardens, and one of them told me about... Nessie."

Jared tried putting a calming hand on her shoulders, but she shrugged him off.

"Want to tell us more about it?" he said gently, his voice full of incubus charm.

Macey sighed. Saying it aloud was going to make it more real.

"He said my late uncle is my father. Which means

that - unless he slept with my mum which I highly doubt - that Nessie is my mother."

"What the..." Cam bit down a string of curses, before he took a deep breath and smoothed his expression. "You don't look like Nessie though."

"I don't look like my mum either. Nor like my dad. Nor like anyone in my family."

"But Nessie is old," Jared mused. "She shouldn't be able to have a child at that age."

Macey sighed. "Kelpies can have children for a lot longer than humans. Almost until they die, pretty much. So, it's definitely possible. But... no, it can't be true. Why would they lie to me? Why would she give me to her sister?"

Tears were running down her face before she even realised that she was crying. Three pairs of arms wrapped themselves around her and she breathed in the scent of her men. It was comforting and sooth-ing. But she wasn't sure she wanted to be soothed right now. She wanted to be angry, and keep that anger burning until she got the chance to confront Nessie.

Her aunt? Her mother? Someone not related to her at all? Macey was beginning to doubt it all. She'd grown up as the third in line to the throne, but if she wasn't her father's daughter, she'd be in a completely different position. And her brothers... maybe they were actually her cousins? That at least would explain why they'd always been so different compared to her.

"Urghhhh!" she groaned, clutching her head in frustration. This couldn't be real. Maybe it was a dream after all?

"Take a deep breath," Jared said softly. "We'll work this out. How about you tell us what else they said?"

Macey noticed she hadn't actually told them all the important bits. The ones that affected all the Wardens, not just herself.

She sighed. "You better get the others while I put on some clothes. We have a lot to discuss.

IZBAN AND AMBER both looked flushed and happy when they joined the other four. Macey hoped they'd actually got some sleep and hadn't just talked, kissed or done other things. They were all going to need their energy.

When they'd all settled down on the bed - which seemed to have grown since the last time she'd slept in it - Macey told them what had happened in her vision.

"You're sure it wasn't just a dream?" Izban asked but Amber elbowed him in the ribs.

"Sorry," he muttered and Amber gave Macey a

cheeky smile. It was good to see that the beithir was dealing with Izban's grumpiness. Maybe he'd actually become bearable now that he had a girlfriend.

"That Warden didn't really seem to be all that useful," Cam observed. "We already knew that the Staran were disintegrating and that it would have terrible effects on everything. Maybe he expanded on how bad it really would be, but he didn't tell us anything about how to stop it, right?"

Macey shook her head. "No, he didn't have any advice. All he said was that now that all seven of us are together, we have a chance. And that the marks are important but we don't need them yet. So, I have time to get my missing ones."

She shot Izban a meaningful look. It was supposed to tell him that she expected him to come up with a solution that didn't involve him sleeping with her or attacking her. The mage seemed clever, so surely he could find a way.

"The appearing thrones didn't make much sense either. Why would we need stone thrones in the future? I don't think the Staran will heal themselves by us looking regal."

Amber chuckled. "I quite like that none of us are human, though. That gives us an advantage over the previous Wardens. It has to count for something, there has to be a reason why suddenly supernaturals became the new Wardens."

Macey nodded. "The humans were only given their elemental power when they became a Warden. They had to learn how to use it. We already know how to, and we all have additional abilities. Amber and I can shift, Izban can do magic and has his little blue helper, Cam and Flint can travel the Staran and Jared... can have sex."

They all laughed, clearing up some of the tension and worry in Macey's chest.

"I'm a bit worried about the internal battles he spoke about," she admitted once they'd calmed down. "I think I can deal with outside battles better than with internal ones."

Amber chuckled bitterly. "I've had my share of internal battles these past few months. If I have to go through something like that again... I'm not sure I'll be able to cope."

Izban put an arm around his partner and pulled her close. She laid her head on his shoulder and closed her eyes.

Macey was hurting for her friend. It was obvious how vulnerable Amber was beneath her strong exterior. The girl wasn't going to keep up the pretense forever. They needed to get this over with before Amber crashed.

"We can help you both," Cam said, interrupting the uncomfortable silence that had fallen over the Wardens.

It was only then Macey realised Luch was missing. Where had the pesky mouse got to? And after the ex-Warden in her dream had revealed such interesting things about her role in fixing the Staran. Though Macey had no idea what actually entail. Hopefully the woman herself would know.

"I know you can," Macey acknowledged. "But that doesn't actually change what happened. We can make ourselves stronger but healing our scars will take longer."

She exchanged a supportive glance with Amber, who smiled weakly. As much as she hated what the Voice had done to both of them, and wished it hadn't happened, she was glad she had someone else who could understand completely.

In time, the two of them would heal. But for now, it was better to repress the nightmares and the negative stuff surrounding them and concentrate on the task at hand.

"That's not a plan for now, though," Amber said, echoing Macey's thoughts.

"Where were the Staran created?" Macey asked absentmindedly. It might not make a difference. But often they said that the best way to fix something was to go to where the root of the problem was. It sounded like the right kind of plan to her. At least it gave them some kind of direction.

"No one really knows, but there's many rumours about it," Cam said.

"Don't tell me, Mount Olympus?" Macey asked, hoping to the very depth of the seas that she was wrong. As much as she wouldn't mind a quick trip to Greece, the thought terrified her. If most of what the humans thought was mere mythology existed in Scotland, then there was going to be some seriously bad things in the other country, and she didn't fancy her chances against sirens or minotaurs.

"No, not Olympus, you'll be glad to know that it literally is just a mountain," Cam said, sounding a little amused. At least her question had raised some spirits then. That was a start.

"So where?"

"This tiny island in the middle of the Northern Sea," Cam answered.

"Because that's a perfectly reasonable place for a travel system to be born," Izban muttered.

"Where would you pick? Somewhere obvious that anyone could find?" Cam bit back.

"Boys," Amber barked. "This is not the time to start arguing. Yes, Izban, it's a weird place. But Cam, he does have a point. If you're going to make something for people to travel on, don't you want them to actually be able to find it?"

"I suppose?" Cam seemed uneasy about the beithir's commanding tone.

"No, not supposing. The answer is yes. You don't put something on a tiny island unless you *don't* want people to find it." Amber rose to her feet and began to pace. "Which raises the question of why."

"But why wouldn't the creator want people to find them?" Macey asked. "Especially when there are other entry points. I mean, they're all over the place," she added, thinking back over all the times they'd travelled on them already.

"My guess is that they were never meant to be used by that. Maybe the person who created them, wanted to be the only person that could. And whenever they landed somewhere, they created another door? It would then open up the Staran to other people then too." Amber's tail swished from side to side as she paced, almost like it was thinking itself.

"She's not completely wrong," Luch said from the doorway, leaning on the frame and studying them all.

"Where does the completely come in?" Macey asked, wondering how long the mouse had been stood there.

"Assuming that it was just one person that created the Staran. They were originally a Unseelie invention. A way for them to travel around the world unchecked by everyone else. They just didn't catch on to the fact that a Seelie woman would uncover their plot. She changed the Staran, and opened them up to the world in general. Or at least, those of us who can see them." She looked straight at Macey, as if knowing she was one of the people that couldn't see them on their own.

"Are the Seelie really that powerful?" Amber asked, turning around so she faced the mouse. And, for the first time since raising to her feet, she stood still. Even her tail wasn't moving anymore.

"Not anymore, no," Luch admitted. "Their powers are constantly weakening. I think a part of them is tied to the Staran, and it's dying off along with it." She sounded sad. Not that Macey knew what she was going to do about that.

"Or is it the other way around?" Macey asked. "Are the Seelie weakening because the Staran are?"

Luch considered her words for a moment. "Possible. Or it could be as simple as an imbalance between the Seelie and Unseelie Courts. No one, even they, aren't sure how the balance actually works."

"One question," Flint interrupted. "What's this got to do with us?"

Everyone turned to face him, and Macey added a questioning look. She had no idea what he was trying to get at.

Flint shrugged. "We're not Seelie or Unseelie. In fact, we're hardly anything but a bunch of misfits. What do we have do with their Courts and the battle between good and bad?"

"It's not a battle," Luch corrected. "It's a balance.

Just like the elements you all represent are all about balance. The world couldn't survive without fire. Nor without water, or air, or any of the others. To think that the two things aren't connected is a failure on your parts. This world is nothing but connections."

Flint nodded. "Okay then, that does make a little bit of sense."

"It makes a lot of sense," Macey added. "Except that there's seven of us."

"Balance can be had between any number," Luch pointed out. "For example, are you not balanced within the Wardens as two relationships? Everyone has someone else they can rely on. No one is left on their own."

"So, it's normal for relationships to occur within the Wardens?" Macey asked softly, wondering what that could mean for them all. Did it take away from their relationship if they were predestined to be?

"It happens," Luch shrugged. "But it's not a given. Sometimes the Wardens hate each other and only come together if they absolutely must. It's very rare for all six of the Wardens to be in a relationship."

"If the Seelie know what's going on with the Staran, why didn't they want us to come and help? They could have told us about their origin, about where to find them. Why didn't they?"

"The woman who helped us said something about evil reaching their queendom," Cam mentioned.

"Maybe they're no longer all on the same side. Maybe the Unseelie have more influence in their court than the balance should allow."

"It seems we have to do it on our own," Flint said with a huff. "Yet again, it's all down to us. Why can't people just be nice and give us some more information?"

Luch chuckled. "It's not in people's nature to be helpful. Nor is it in that of mice." She grinned cheekily. "But I'm an exception. I'm nice, so I'm going to tell you where to go. It's a pretty place, actually, I haven't been in years. I'm going to think of this as a holiday. You can do the work and I'll enjoy the scenery."

Macey grimaced. Luch was proving once again that the mouse knew far more than she let on.

"Where is it?" she asked.

"St Kilda. The last islands before there's nothing until you reach America. An archipelago with the highest sea cliffs in all of Britain. It's a beautiful set of islands, you'll like it."

"Is anyone still living there?" Jared asked and Luch tsked.

"Don't you know your history, incubus? The last humans left in 1930. Until then, the islands had been inhabited for over two thousand years. Long enough for the people there to grow used to guarding the Staran. But over time, their tasks became legends and the younger generations no longer knew what to do. So, the Staran became weaker, missing the monthly rituals that kept it pure and alive. Missionaries arrived in the middle ages, and while spreading their religious message, they also destroyed some of the knowledge that had been collected about the Staran and the island's mythological origins."

"How do you know all that?" Macey was impressed by the mouse's knowledge, but at the same time, she was wondering why she hadn't told them before.

"I know a lot more, but it's not time yet to divulge all my secrets. Once our story comes closer to its end, I will. I promise."

"Does that mean we have to go to St Kilda now?" Amber asked. Tiredness had left dark shadows below her eyes, but she was smiling in excitement.

"I think I'd like to have a chat with Nessie first. She's got a lot to explain," Macey growled, failing to hide the anger once again bubbling up in her. The talk of the Staran and St Kilda had almost distracted her from the big revelation about her family, but she was not getting it quite out of her mind, and she was sure she wouldn't until she'd confronted her aunt... or whatever Nessie was to her.

"I'm not sure we'll have time," Izban began but Amber elbowed him again.

"Put yourself in Macey's shoes," the beithir

scoffed. "Wouldn't you want to know as well? I don't think she'll be able to focus on anything until she finds out if Nessie is her mother."

There was no accusation in Amber's voice, just sympathy. Macey gave her a thankful smile.

"Do you think the Staran can get us to her or are they too weak?" Izban asked the two wraiths and Macey's smile disappeared. She could see the barb in the mage's question. He was trying to make her feel guilty for using the Staran and she didn't like that at all. Maybe because in her mind, she knew he was right, while hear heart was telling her to race to Nessie without delay.

"We could split up," Macey suggested diplomatically. "I could go find Nessie and then join you on St Kilda. Although I'd need Cam or Flint to help me travel."

"No, all of you need to be there together," Luch said sternly. "It won't work otherwise."

"What won't work?" Cam asked, suspicion lacing his voice. "What aren't you telling us?"

Luch didn't even look embarrassed or uncomfortable. She just shrugged and said, "I've told you too much already. I've been helping you more than I should. So, don't ask me any more questions, just believe me when I say that all of you need to arrive on Hirta together."

"Hirta?"

Luch sighed. "So, you don't just need to brush up on your history, but also on geography. It's the largest island in the St Kilda archipelago and our destination. It's where the very first Warden lived, before it was decided that more than one was needed. Her house, the *Taigh na Banaghaisgeich*, is where we want to go."

"But what about Nessie?" Macey asked quietly. Her wish for personal closure was fighting her need to help the Wardens. Was this the first inner battle she'd been warned about? Or was a lot worse to come?

"Once we're done exploring St Kilda, you may have more things to discuss with Nessie," Luch said, and Macey was tempted to strangle her. How many more mysteries and unanswered questions were there going to be?

Yes, she was in the mood to go to an island, but one with beaches and sun and peace, where she could stretch out and read, maybe sleep a little, play on the sand with her men. Not an island full of legends and problems.

It took all her inner strength to bury her desire to talk to - or better, confront - Nessie and instead focus on the greater good.

"Let's go," she said and got up before she could change her mind. Let's go to Hirta."

ST KILDA SONG.

Sleeps he in your breezy shade
Ye rocks with moss and ivy waving,
On some bank where wild waves laving,
Murmur through the twisted willow?
On that bank, O were I laid,
How soft should be my lover's pillow!

13

St Kilda looked a bit like Macey imagined Avalon. A group of green islands, shrouded in mist. High cliffs were rising from the sea, where foamy waves were battering the dark stone. Tiny white dots signaled the presence of sheep who'd somehow stayed behind when the last residents were evacuated. Seabirds, mainly gulls and gannets, were circling far overhead, curiously looking down at the newcomers.

Tourists came here regularly, that much was clear from the information boards and the metal bin by the pier, but right now, there didn't seem to be anyone else on the island.

They'd stepped out of the Staran in the imaginatively named Village Bay, at least that's what it said on the map Macey was looking at.

Some of the stone houses around them had turned into ruins, but some still looked habitable, with complete roofs and unbroken windows. Somewhere here was the *Taigh na Banaghaisgeich,* the female warrior's house. Oh yes, there it was. The map called it the Amazon's House, which was intriguing. Macey wouldn't have associated a remote Scottish archipelago with a warrior woman.

It probably wasn't even anyone Scottish that had named the place. It sounded like the kind of thing a foreigner would have come up with.

"This way," Flint said, turning them up a small dirt track to the left.

"How do you know?" Macey huffed, feeling terribly unfit. She was going to blame her stint in the Voice's keep for that. She'd been in much better shape before that. Though she hadn't shifted properly since they'd been at the ceasg's home, and that hardly counted. She hadn't been in kelpie form for long, and she'd been fighting for Amber's life. Or thought she had been. The exact details of that were a little hazy.

"I don't know, just a feeling."

She didn't like that idea much. Feelings had normally turned out to be bad so far. And ended in them being trapped places they shouldn't, with people who got angry at them for the oddest of reasons.

Even so, she stuck with it, and they all climbed the very basic path without saying a word. Too much concentration was needed to navigate the rocky path. Why no one kept it clearer of the pebbles and other debris that were strewn over it, Macey had no idea. It was like everything about this world was out to get them.

"It's a pile of stones," Jared huffed as the Amazon's house came into view.

Macey didn't voice her opinion out loud, but she couldn't help but agree with Jared. It *was* just a pile of stones. Though she could see where the house would once have stood. It was a shame really, the shape of it made it seem like the structure would have been a sight to behold.

"Oh ye of little faith," Luch said, amusement colouring her voice.

She cleared her throat and opened her mouth, music beginning the moment she did so. Macey stared in awe at the mouse. This was the last thing she'd expected.

"By the steam so cool and clear,
And thro' the caves where breezes languish,
Soothing still my tender anguish,
Hoping still to find my lover,
I have wander'd far and near:
O where shall I the youth discover?"

By the time Luch had finished the verse, tears were falling down her face, as she watched the place where the home had once stood. Her expression changed from one of sadness, to joy.

Confused, Macey turned back to the ruins, only to discover a beautiful stone building rising in front of them. It was simple in appearance, but clearly built with love and care. The doorway was arched, created from interlocking stones, and it hardly looked as if it had been touched by time at all. It was exactly the kind of thing Macey had expected, just with a few centuries less of weathering.

> "Sleeps he in your breezy shade,
> Ye rocks with moss and ivy waving,
> On some bank where wild waves laving,
> Murmur through the twisted willow?
> On that bank, O were I laid,
> How soft should be my lover's pillow!"

Macey jumped as the male voice replied to Luch's song. It wasn't what she'd expected. It had an ethereal note to it. Almost like Fedelm when she'd been speaking. But that would mean...

"Bradaigh," Luch exclaimed, jumping into action and running down to the entrance of the Amazon's home.

Macey followed her down, not at all surprised to

find her greeting a translucent man. A man who was looking at Luch like she was the only woman in the world.

"It's been a long time, Luch," the man said now he'd stopped singing.

"I'm sorry, Bradaigh. It's taken me this long to find them," Luch replied, reaching her hand up as if to try and touch the ghostly face of the man.

"I know, I've been watching when I can. Except from when you were in that horrible dark place." He shuddered, sending a shimmering light through him. It was an odd thing to watch. Almost like sunlight when it rippled through the surface of the water back in Macey's Loch.

How she missed that place. Before her adventure, it had seemed small and confining. Now, she almost wished she was back in the cool, calm waters, surrounding by the people she'd known since birth. Even if that did mean facing Aunt Nessie again. The only thing stopping her from running right back home and denying anything had ever happened, was the fact she wouldn't have her men if things had gone any differently.

"I'm sorry, it had to be done. I'm protecting us now," Luch said, nodding furiously. Bradaigh nodded.

"I can tell. I'd recognise one of your shields anywhere." He stroked the tip of his finger down Luch's cheek, though they didn't actually touch.

Macey's heart broke for the two of them. There was so much love on display between them, and yet it couldn't be realised. Not unless Luch suddenly learned how to make herself into a spirit. If anyone knew how, it'd be the mouse. Though Macey suspected she'd already have done it if she could.

"These are them?" he asked.

"Yes, these are the newest Wardens," Luch said.

Macey grimaced slightly at the use of newest. She didn't like the fact there'd been so many Wardens before them. Or that they were nothing more than another set in a long line. Even so, the seven of them were unique. They were the first Wardens made up of all supernatural beings. That was a start. If she kept reminding herself of that, then she wouldn't feel too bad about being just the next set.

"And you brought a kelpie? Are you crazy?" Bradaigh demanded.

"After all these years, you're still not going to let go of that stupid prejudice? We both know that neither of your kinds are responsible for it. That has Unseelie written all over it," Luch admonished him.

"It's not about my own prejudices. I couldn't care less. You know as well as I do, that I've known for thousands of years the importance of the Wardens. I'm not going to turn my nose up at her just because she's a kelpie. But the others..." he trailed off.

Macey hissed, and glared at him. There'd only be

one creature that talked that way, and she didn't like that he was one of them at all. Though it did explain the song, and the reason this place was so deserted.

"They wouldn't come here, would they?" Luch asked, a slight quiver in her voice that Macey wasn't a fan of at all. Anything that scared the mouse was certainly a bad thing.

"They always get in the way."

No, that quiver in Luch's voice hadn't been fear. It had been annoyance. Anger. The mouse didn't seem to like the other selkies, even though her lover was that species. There was no doubt that the two of them were deeply in love. It made it even more heartbreaking to see the women, made of flesh and blood, and the man, a ghostly figure who couldn't touch her. She hoped the two of them had had a good life before Bradaigh became a spirit. A ghost. Whatever he was. The alternative was too sad to even imagine.

Macey tried hard not to cry and the sight of them. It was one of the most heartbreaking and depressing things she'd ever seen. And one of the most touching.

"Would you like to introduce us?" she asked gently, trying to get back to work before her unshed tears escaped her.

They both turned away from each other, but their hands stayed close, almost touching.

"This is Bradaigh, my husband," Luch explained. "He's not a Warden, but as my companion, he was bestowed the same eternal life that all Wardens get rewarded with."

"Wait, you were a Warden too?" Flint asked, saying what Macey had just thought.

"Yes, once, a long time ago. I am no longer, of course, there are only ever one set of Wardens. Back when it was my turn, it was just me. A lone Warden, tending to the Staran, living all by myself in this little house. They chose me because I was unattached, without family who would miss me if something went awry with the transformation. I was the first, you see? They didn't know if their plans would actually work."

"Who's they?"

Bradaigh looked at his wife in confusion. "You've not told them?"

"I wanted to make sure they were ready," Luch replied softly. "Shall we go inside? If we're lucky, there's still some peat we can use to make ourselves some tea."

Macey turned to her fellow Wardens. They seemed just as stunned as she felt. Luch, a Warden. The first one. Who turned out to be married to a ghost. It was all a bit much. She breathed in the cold, salty air to clear her head.

"I'm not sure what's going on," Jared muttered. "There's so much she could have told us before, but instead, she brought us here. I'm not sure we can trust her."

"I disagree," Amber suddenly said. "Her feelings for him are true. So is what she said to him. We weren't ready before. We had to see this house reappear. We had to see where she's from before we could believe who she is." She smiled, removing some of the gravitas from her words. "Shall we go inside? I'd kill for a cup of tea right now."

Luckily, Amber didn't have to kill anyone. Luch managed to start a fire in the simple hearth using a heap of old peat, before asking Macey to conjure some water to fill the kettle. The peat smoke slowly began to fill the house, a warming, comfortable scent that made it smell like a home. A place where people lived, not one that was solely inhabited by a ghost waiting for his wife.

Bradaigh was sitting on a bench, not taking his eyes off Luch. He took in her every move with a longing that made Macey's heart ache for them once again. She suddenly understood Luch's brusque manner a lot more.

"I haven't met a kelpie in ages," he suddenly said, turning to Macey who had slipped onto the bench next to him.

"I've never met a selkie," she admitted. "But I've not heard many good things about your kind."

She instantly regretted saying that. He seemed like a nice man and she really didn't want to offend him.

Luckily, he chuckled. "I've not heard many good things about your kind, either. But I've met and befriended kelpies, which is a lot more important than hearsay and rumours, wouldn't you say?"

Macey nodded. "I met a ceasg recently and had only ever heard terrible, frightening tales about them. It turned out she was really nice and helpful."

"Oh, there are not many ceasg around anymore. You're lucky to have met one." He laughed again. "There are a lot of selkies though, they live all around St Kilda. You may want to stay away from them; most of them have never met a kelpie before and all they've heard about you are legends of how you drown and eat humans."

"I'm a vegetarian," Macey said automatically, and he grinned.

"So am I. It's very amusing to see someone else use that argument."

"I should really know better by now," Macey berated herself, annoyed that she hadn't really thought to question her thoughts and feelings towards selkies before now.

Of all the creatures she'd met along the way, almost none of them had turned out to be anything like what the rumours and tales had said.

Probably the humans fault. She imagined a human must have drowned in a loch where kelpies lived, and they'd taken the blame. Or maybe it was worse than that. Maybe it was humans killing other humans and blaming it on the myths of old. That wouldn't surprise her. Not from what she' seen of the misrepresented creatures.

"Please explain more," she prompted, after taking a sip of her tea. She aimed the question at Luch. While debating why kelpies and selkies had been led to hate one another was interesting, it didn't get them any further on their quest to save the Staran.

Luch sighed. "Which bit do you want explaining first?" she asked.

"Start with who you mean by they?" Macey prompted, hoping that was the right thing to ask first. It was hard to tell what questions she should be asking when she had absolutely no idea of any of the answers. In some ways, it was easier to question the things that had happened already. That way, she had something to ground her answers on.

"The gods," Luch said with a shrug.

"The gods don't exist," Macey blurted.

"Really?" Amber questioned. "After all that we've been through, you're going to question the existence of gods?"

"And you're not? Are beithirs brought up believing in them?" Macey demanded, though not unkindly. She didn't want to start a disagreement with her friend. She just wanted to get to the bottom of it all.

"No, we're not. But after all we've seen and done, including the mysteriously appearing marks on your back, are gods really too much of a stretch?"

Macey slumped back in her seat, and took a sip of her tea, letting the warm liquid slip down her throat and soothe her in a way nothing else could. It was one of her favourite things about being above water.

Well, other than her other three favourite things. She looked between her men, noting they were listening intently. They were learning new things too then. That made a change. They always seemed to be telling her things, and adding to her knowledge. And quite frankly, making her feel like the naive and sheltered loch kelpie that she was slowly learning she actually was. It had been a hard lesson to learn, but she liked to believe she was strong for it.

"No. Gods aren't too much of a stretch," Macey added. "Where are they now?" she asked Luch.

"Dead. Gone. On vacation. I'm not really sure. But I don't think they're about, if that's what you're getting at."

Macey nodded along. That made sense. There was very little point to having gods involved if they were just going to solve everything. Oh no. That would be way too easy.

"They created the Wardens to do the job they're supposed to do themselves, didn't they?" Amber asked.

One glance over at her friend showed just how uncomfortable she was. She was nestled into Izban's shoulder, his arm wrapped tightly around her. But it was her tail that gave everything away. It was curled up in Amber's lap, switching slightly as she stroked it.

No. Amber was particularly uncomfortable with what was happening.

Macey didn't blame her. She couldn't say she was a fan of how complicated things had become. And she'd be even less so if she'd been kidnapped from school, locked up, and then instantly thrown into this situation, like Amber had. In fact, they all deserved a decent rest when all of this was over.

"I think so," Luch responded. "But I'm not sure. For the first hundred years or so, I did exactly what I was told. And then something changed. I'm still not sure what it was, but I think someone else tried to tamper with the Staran, and I got caught out. It sucked, but there was very little I could do. It was shortly after that when the gods decided I wasn't enough. They created the Seven Wardens and tasked me to watch over them."

"But?" Macey prompted. She could hear that it existed just from the mouse's tone. She just hoped Luch would actually tell them what she meant, and not just keep them in the dark like she had been.

"I'm not sure. That first set of Wardens did every-thing they were supposed to do, when they were supposed to do it. But something didn't quite work out. The same happened for the second set, and the third..." she trailed off, then shrugged. "You get the picture."

"Basically, you're saying that even when the Wardens know what to do, it ends up going wrong?" Jared asked.

"Not wrong, wrong. What they do works, otherwise the Staran would have disappeared years ago. But it's not stabilised everything quite the way it should," Bradaigh answered.

"Is that because the issue is bigger than the Staran themselves?"

"Yes and no," Luch answered.

"The Seven Wardens job is to stabilise the Staran. And yes, before you ask, I will tell you how to go about doing that," Luch said, holding up a hand to stop Flint from speaking.

It wasn't Flint Macey was concerned about though. Cam had been suspiciously quiet through the entire conversation, causing worry to build within her. He was normally so aware of everything that was going on, and the fact that he wasn't, was somewhat concerning.

"Why do I feel like there's another but coming?" Jared joked.

"There is. I don't think your job as Wardens is going to just include the Staran. I think you need to stabilise something far, far bigger than that." Luch worried her hands together, as if she was nervous to admit whatever it was.

"Let's guess," Macey started. "All we have to do is save the world?"

Luch gave a dry laugh. "Something like that, yes."

"How about we focus on one problem at a time?" Cam said gravely. He looked as exhausted as Macey felt. "Can we fix the Staran first and then worry about the rest of the world later?"

"I'm afraid you won't be able to repair the Staran entirely without looking at the bigger picture. They would only destabilise again," Luch replied with a sad smile.

"But how long will we be able to continue travelling on the Staran? We already need one of the wraiths," Jared protested. "What if we repair them and then fix whatever else needs to be fixed immediately afterwards? Would that work?"

Bradaigh nodded thoughtfully. "It should, yes. The Staran won't destabilise that quickly. How long do they still have, love?"

"No more than three weeks. I can feel the end coming ever closer. There's not much time left."

"How do we do it?" Cam asked, directing his question at Luch. "How long will it take?"

Luch sighed. "When I said that I'd tell you how to do it, I meant I'd tell you what I assume. It's all a rough guess, if you will, but usually my guesses turn out to be right."

"I can vouch for that," Bradaigh said with a chuckle. "She's almost always right."

"Almost?!"

He cleared his throat. "Ehm... always?"

"Good. Now, as you know, the origin of the Staran is here on St Kilda. The problem is that it's hidden deep beneath the island. Back when I was guarding them, it was a cave that could be accessed through a long tunnel when the tide was out. But since then, the sea has claimed the cave and it's now permanently underwater. Which means that only one of you will be able to go there. Two, if you count Air as Macey's stowaway."

"No way. Macey is not going there on her own," Flint protested immediately. "The water is dangerous."

Macey put an arm on his shoulders, soothing him. "The water isn't dangerous to me. I've grown up underwater, I've spent more years there than above ground. Don't worry about me, I've always wanted to explore a proper sea cave."

She turned to Luch. "What will await me down there? What do I need to do?"

"The Staran is fueled by a jewel filled with the energy the gods provided for it," the woman explained. "It was supposed to be enough for thousands of years, so I doubt it's been depleted. Maybe there's something blocking its access. If it's something you can't fix yourself, just swim back up and we'll talk it through."

That sounded easy enough. Water was her element and she wasn't afraid of it. The cave didn't sound very scary either. If there was only a jewel down there, it couldn't be much of a threat. Unless there were selkies... Bradaigh had said that they frequented these waters. All Macey could hope was that she'd be able to avoid a confrontation with them.

"Good, let's do this," Macey announced, unwilling to lose any more time. The quicker they could get this over with, the quicker they'd be able to get some rest. And there was still a chat to be had with Nessie.

LUCH LED them back down to the beach and along a path that led to a high cliff. She pointed towards the sea.

"The entrance is about fifty metres that way. I hope it hasn't collapsed when it was flooded, but it should be fine. The tunnel itself will be narrow, so be sure to stay clear of the sharp rocks on the ceiling. It usually took me around ten minutes to reach the large cave in the centre. There you'll find the jewel. I hope."

Macey stripped, prompting Flint to growl at

Izban and Bradaigh to turn around. She waded into the cold water until it reached her shoulders, shivering at the same time as rejoicing in the feel of the waves surrounding her body. Finally, she was going to be able to swim again. It had been too long.

She turned back to the others who were waiting on the beach. Jared gave her a cheery thumbs up and she laughed before shifting in one fluid motion. Once her gills developed on her neck, she let herself drop into the water, breathing in deep. She always felt like she got more oxygen underwater than up above. Her gills seemed more effective than her human lungs.

With a strong stride of her tail, she swam in the direction Luch had shown her. The ocean floor beneath her slowly turned from rocks and sand to a lively home. Tiny fish were zipping past her while large algae gently stroked her skin as she swam past them.

After so long without shifting, this was heavenly. She whinnied in delight and almost forgot she had a task to do. She could have swum here for hours, if she'd had the time to do so. It was a beautiful world underwater, and the water was so much clearer here than in her loch back home. Intense pinks, greens and oranges were offset by the rich turquoise water. She couldn't take her eyes off the ocean floor and all the plants and fish living there.

Macey almost missed the cave entrance; it was

that hidden beneath a dense kelp forest and carpets of iridescent jewel anemones, literally hundreds of thousands clinging onto the cliff faces and boulders. She smiled at the beauty of it.

With her front hooves, she pulled apart the kelp and squeezed inside. The stone tunnel was darker than the sea outside, but still light enough to see. The walls were covered with incredibly dense thickets of hydroids, who themselves provided shelter for what must have been literally millions of tiny shrimps. The ground was smooth, probably worn down by the effect of the waves reaching in and out during the tides.

Macey made a mental note to explore all the caves beneath St Kilda one day. She was sure there were more than just this one, and if even half of them were as beautiful, she wanted to see them.

She took her time, taking in the shimmering tunnel walls and the algae covering the ground. The kelp was only growing outside where it got some sunlight filtering through the water, but there was none of that in here.

Far too soon though, the tunnel widened and opened into a large cavern. The water temperature changed as soon as she exited the tunnel. Warm water surrounded her, making her feel as if she'd entered a giant bathtub. She shook her body, letting the warmth penetrate her scales. So comfy...

Kelpies didn't mind cold water, but she could certainly appreciate how lovely warm water could be.

The sea didn't fill the entire cavern, so to make it easier to survey the place, Macey took a deep breath and lifted her head above water. She almost gasped when she took in the sight in front of her.

At the end of the cave, a stone pedestal rose from the water, and on it was the largest crystal she'd ever seen. It was egg-shaped but almost as tall as a kelpie foal. And it was glittering in hundreds of colours.

She dived back underwater, deciding that she'd have to shift again to be able to inspect the crystal. She'd be naked, but who was going to see her down here anyway? The sponges and shrimps didn't seem to care.

St Kilda

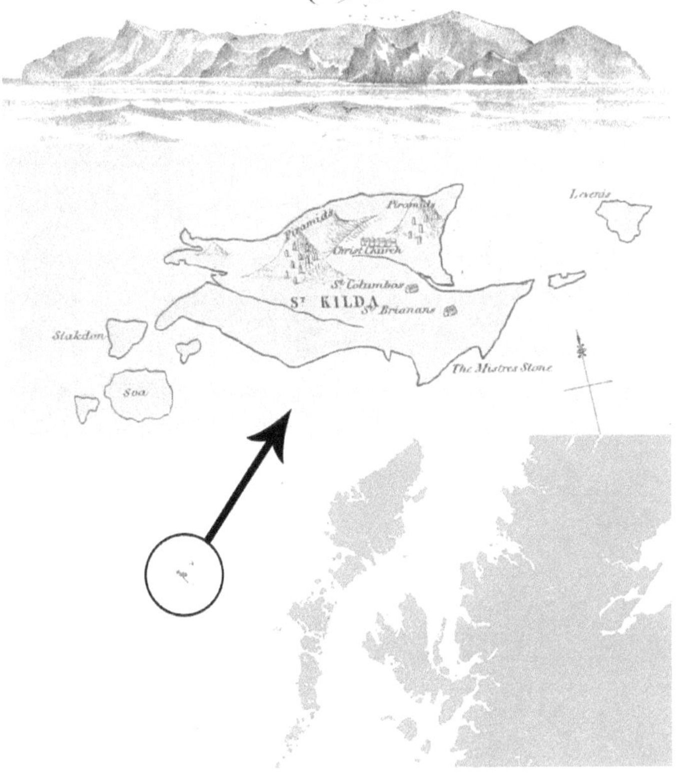

St. Kilda

She wasn't sure if it was just sheer exhaustion, or if shifting was actually getting easier. But this time, it didn't hurt as much as it had in the past.

Now in human form, she was glad for the warmth of the water, and the way it was enveloping her, making her feel kind of safe and secure, probably for the first time in weeks. Macey knew it was just an illusion, but she was going to enjoy it nonetheless.

The currents pushed against Macey as she walked through it. This was a definite drawback of being in her human form. What wasn't, was the way her eyesight worked. Her kelpie eyes were designed to see the underwater tones, and that meant they couldn't see quite so well above the surface. But now, as a human, she could see everything so clearly. The colours coming from the crystal glittered against the walls, showering the cave in a rainbow of light.

It was bouncing off the water too, which only added to the atmosphere around her.

Macey really wished her men could see this and didn't quite understand why they couldn't. All they'd need would be an enchantment like the storm kelpies had around their heads, and they'd be able to breathe underwater and join her here.

The only answer must have been magic. Only one person could enter, because that was all the gods had decided could.

Macey scoffed. The gods indeed. She couldn't even work out where they fit in. Or why everyone was so convinced they didn't exist, when they actually did. Or had. She wasn't all that clear on that one.

Shaking her head to clear it of any errant thoughts, Macey refocused on the task at hand, striding forward through the water, finding it easier going as it became shallower, the soft waves lapping against her ankles.

The rock floor of the cave was slightly scratchy against her bare feet, but she ignored it. That was really the least of her problems. Her legs burned as she climbed the naturally occurring steps, each one taking her closer to the crystal at the top.

Talia? she called in her head, hoping Air would hear her and respond, but knowing that wasn't likely to be the case. Air had explained that wasn't how it worked, but so far, Macey hadn't seen any of the other Warden's powers manifest in herself.

As she suspected, there was no response from the Warden. Macey guessed she was doing this alone then.

She reached the top of the staircase and found herself level with the pedestal. Reverently, she walked towards it, unsure what to do with herself.

The lights dancing off it only grew brighter as she approached, and she remembered something her Aunt had said when she was younger. She'd called them fairy lights. Dancing against the walls and doors of the palace underwater. It was even more spectacular here. Probably because light behaved differently above the surface of the water.

Macey frowned. Where even was the light coming from? She looked upwards, eager to know the answer, and was relieved to find a small chimney-like hole above her head. That explained the air too. She wasn't likely to suffocate down here, though with her ability to shift, that wasn't really a possibility anyway.

Not sure if it was what she was supposed to do, Macey reached out and placed her hands on the stone. It lit up far more brightly than it had before, and something opened up in her mind.

Images fluttered past her now closed eyes, showing Macey the journeys of the other past

Wardens, as well as other creatures who lived around and about these parts. It was a wonder to behold. There was so much culture in this one spot, and she gained a new understanding of the world.

But not of the Staran. She could feel them screaming out to her, and wanting to be healed, but not knowing how. She could even sense them trying to repair the damage that had been done to them.

Tears pooled in Macey's eyes as she felt the pain they had been going through. And it wasn't just the past few months of pain, but years. Decades. Centuries even. This problem was going a lot further back than anyone had even realised.

No wonder the Wardens hadn't managed to fix the Staran. They were acting as more of a band aid than a cure. And therein lay the problem. No one had looked into it. Maybe no one had even be able to sense it. That would make some kind of warped sense, considering the past Wardens had been humans.

That must be the link if her own set were all supernatural. Hope welled up within her. Maybe this meant they really did stand a chance at fixing things. Or maybe not. Maybe they were doomed like every other set of Wardens before them.

Macey dug around inside the connection between her and the crystal, searching for whatever it was that was blocking the Staran from healing themselves.

Finding what appeared to be a rotten part of the line, she mentally followed it, picking up pieces of the healthy Staran and trying to use them to knit everything back together at the same time. Nothing seemed to hold though, leaving it unraveling behind her and leaving the Staran in the same mess as they were before, but thankfully not worse.

Why was this happening? Luch had implied that Macey would know what to do when she was faced with the Staran themselves. Yet, here she was, and she was as confused as ever.

She continued following them down the apparently rotten path, not finding much more to do, but feeling this was her best choice.

After a few moments, something black and foreboding formed in her way, and somehow, she knew this was what was causing all the issues. All she had to do now was work out how to undo it.

Stealing herself mentally, Macey began to poke at the dark mass, turning it around in her head to try and locate its weak points.

Or she did, until a tremor beneath her feet tore her from her task. She steadied herself against the pedestal, while glancing around frantically and trying to ignore the panic welling up inside her.

There was nothing to be seen. No cracks in the walls, no intruder, not even a ripple in the water. She put her hands back on the crystal. It was vibrating slightly. Had it done that before? No, she was sure it hadn't. She reached out for the Staran again and the black mass. As soon as she got close to it, the ground started to shake again. This time, she didn't let go of the stone. She was beginning to realise that the shaking wasn't physical. It was in her mind.

Something was fighting back. But Macey had been fighting off the Voice for weeks, if not months. She was experienced in mental fights by now. This shouldn't scare her. It was only another challenge, nothing more. She reached out again, continuing her scan for the black mass's weak spots, but as soon as she seemed to have found something, the thing wobbled and changed its shape. It was continuously turning and twisting, reforming every second or so. How was she supposed to deal with this? She was sure this was the reason for the Staran's disease. A para-site, embedded deep within them.

"How do I get you out of there?" she whispered to herself, struggling to get a grip on it. It was too slippery and slimy. "And how did you get there in the first place?"

At least now she knew what was wrong with the Staran. It was rather easy to see.

She prodded the black blob with her mental fingers. Suddenly, black sparks shot up, forming a line leading out through the hole in the cave ceiling. A moment later, they'd disappeared, but a suspicion was forming in Macey. She prodded it again, and as before, tiny black flecks sparked. It was as if the mass was sending out a call for help. As if it was connected to others of its kind.

Macey focused on the blob again, but this time, she expanded her senses, exploring its surface.

Yes, there it was! A tiny black string, reaching up into the air, disappearing through the hole. She tried following it with her mind but didn't get very far. Still, it was progress.

Now she knew why healing the Staran wouldn't be enough. Even if this blob disappeared, there were others out there. And maybe they'd be able to infect the Staran once again. They needed to find the root of this strange dark power.

But she didn't want to leave here without having at least tried healing them. Otherwise travelling on them would get harder and harder with every day that passed and this black mass was allowed to eat the Staran up from the inside.

Somehow, Macey knew that this wasn't going to be a physical battle. No, this was what had been fore-told: she was going to fight a mental battle, one within herself. Maybe now was the time to feel a little scared, but she was too determined to let fear get in the way.

She took a deep breath and plunged herself into the Staran, head first. Her body stayed behind but her mind flew along the misty stream of power that was the Staran. Lives and memories flashed past her, far more intense than the short glimpse she'd been given earlier. They were too fast to understand, though, no more than whispers and echoes racing past at an astonishing speed.

Was this what it was like for Cam and Flint to travel on the Staran? She'd never asked them but it seemed it was a lot more comfortable for them than for her - when she had her body with her. Right now, it wasn't too bad.

She flew further, searching for the black mass. But it ended up finding her.

Suddenly, she bumped against an invisible barrier and fell to the ground. She was standing on flashes of light, intermixed with splinters of images and memories. There were whispers in the distance, too faint to understand. She looked up, searching for whatever had stopped her flight. There was nothing. Not even a strange shimmer in the air.

The ground rumbled without warning and Macey swayed, reaching out for something to hold on to but there was no pedestal this time. She fell to her hands and knees, for the first time feeling the cool texture of the ground. She'd been on it barefoot - she was naked, after all - but it was different touching it with her fingers. It was like pliable glass, strangely cool and soft at the same time. And pretty.

No, it wasn't. Black lines were forming in front of her, turning into a spiral swirling on the ground until it became a perfect circle. Macey scrambled to her feet and stepped away from the black circle, but once again, something stopped her from moving further away. With her back against the barrier, she watched as the black began to bubble and rise up, becoming three dimensional. A column. No, wait. A person.

She stared in horror as the black mass slowly turned into someone very familiar.

"Hello, darling," the black Macey said and grinned, exposing sharp black teeth.

<h1 style="text-align:center">15</h1>

It was like looking in a mirror. If that mirror was filled with black sludge and didn't quite make any sense.

Macey lifted her left arm, only to see Sludge-Macey do the same. It was disconcerting to say the least.

She closed her eyes for a moment, before opening them, and being disappointed to discover that her opposite was very much still there.

That was annoying. She'd hoped it was just a figment of her imagination. Albeit one that was sitting within her imagination to begin with. She had very little doubt that her version of what the insides of the Staran looked like was different from what they looked like to past Wardens. This was just her interpretation, and she was fine with that.

Opening her eyes, she sighed. Not just a figment of her imagination then. An actual obstacle to overcome. Macey took a deep breath. She could do this.

She could face herself and win.

Even if facing herself was quite possibly the scariest thing she could think of. This was well beyond anything the Voice could do to her. And well beyond any other kind of enemy. This was going to be every doubt, and every fear she had, all rolled into one, and presented in a way that could weaken her to her very core.

"What do you want?" she demanded of herself.

Sludge-Macey giggled. "Everything," it responded.

Macey refused to accept that the thing was her and tried to change it back into a blob in her head. Alas, it did not seem to work.

"Sorry, but that's just not going to be possible."

"Is it not, Macey?" Sludge-Thing said. It even went as far as brushing a strand of its hair behind its ear, smiling as it did.

"No. You can't have anything."

"Not even your three, lovely men. Strong, aren't they? Virile, affectionate. Everything anyone could possibly want from a man. And you get three..."

Macey shivered, not fully aware of where this was going, or how worried she should be. What was this thing's game?

"But I have a question for you," it said.

"What is it?" Macey snapped.

"Why on earth, or on the Staran even, would they love you? You're just a little loch kelpie a long way from home," the thing sneered.

"So?" Macey prompted. "There's nothing wrong with being a loch kelpie. It's not like I had any choice in where I was born." Her thoughts flitted towards Aunt Nessie, but she pushed them to the side. That wasn't the kind of thing she wanted the Sludge-Macey to pick up on.

"Oh, I see where your mind went there," it taunted. "Don't think I don't know your thoughts, Macey."

"If you know my thoughts, then surely you know you're not going to win." Macey tried not to make it sound like a question, but she wasn't completely convinced she'd managed. Oh well, it wasn't like she had any other choice but to go with it any more.

"Oh, Macey, Macey, Macey. Hasn't anyone ever told you that you are always your own worst enemy?" the thing said.

"Then surely I'm also my own best ally." She straightened her spine and faced off against the thing. "You can question how much my men love me, and why, and that's fine. But you can't change that I know it deep down in my soul. They love me with every fibre of their beings. Just like I love them. So, stop questioning something I know is true."

Macey wasn't sure where the words had come from, but they'd burst out of her all of a sudden, and she had absolutely no doubt they were true. Even if Flint was the only one who'd ever said the words out loud. It didn't matter. They loved her. She knew that. Their bond was one that couldn't be broken, even by the anxiety of her own soul.

"If you think your men are your only weak spot, then you're kidding yourself," the thing changed tactics.

"You're right. They're not my only weakness. But I hardly see why that matters. Isn't being brave about doing something despite being scared? Or despite the fact it's not something you're good at?" Macey asked.

All she received in response was stunned silence.

"I will hold up my hands and say I am scared. I'm filled with doubts over whether or not I can do the task that's been assigned to me. A lot of responsibility is on my shoulders, and it is a lot to take. Particularly when I have my own demons to face. But I am damned well going to do it regardless. Failure is not an option and I won't be letting my own little voice defeat me."

She'd ended up shouting the words, but in some ways, was glad for that. It made them ring truer in her own mind. And hopefully to the Sludge-Thing too.

"Oh, Macey. Don't you think you're too weak for

this?" it tried. But even Macey could tell it was beginning to flag.

She had her weaknesses, but she was going to own them. There was really no other choice in her head. This must have been the mental battle the past Warden had mentioned to her. She hadn't even considered that she might have to fight it against herself. The Voice would have been her first guess, but apparently not.

Such an odd thought that she was one of her own worst enemies.

"I am weak, yes. But my strength comes from fighting that," she mused aloud. "I don't know everything, but I have Cam for that. I don't always have it all together, but I have Jared. Flint would do anything to fight for me. I have Amber to be a friend even when I can't be to myself. And I'm not really sure about Izban, but I'm sure he provides something I can't for myself too. Alone, I might be too weak to complete the task that's been set for me. In that, you're correct. But I am not alone. And even if you're really a part of me, you shouldn't be fooling me into thinking that I am alone."

A warm wind rose and touched her skin gently. She smiled.

"And I have Air with me, too. I will never be alone, even though it might seem like that at first.

Now go back to where you came from. I have work to do."

Now it was sludge-Macey's turn to smile. "As you wish," she said with a wicked grin before launching herself at Macey.

Instead of crashing into her, the fake Macey puffed out of existence as soon as she touched her doppelganger. At first, nothing happened, but just when hope began to appear, Macey crumbled to the ground, clutching her head in agony.

"You're not rid of me yet!" a voice inside her mind said, a voice very similar to her own. No, the same. They'd taken their battle from the Staran into her mind. Macey wasn't sure if that was better or worse. At least they couldn't injure the Staran further in here, right? All that could break was her mind... not as important for the fate of the world... she hoped.

"How do I get rid of you?" Macey asked, hoping that the evil her would confide that secret. Somehow, the evil people in stories always did share their plans at some point.

"You do know that I can hear you?" the sludge-Macey sneered. "I know what you think, so don't even try and come up with a plan. I'll know what you intend at the same time as you do. There's no chance of you winning. How about you give in now and stop wasting time?"

"I can't do that. You're hurting the Staran and

through that, you're destroying the lives of supernaturals all over the place. You need to leave."

Sludge-Macey laughed. "And why would I do that? I like it here. It's a comfortable place, and so many lives to feed from. Whenever someone travels through here, I get to see a bit of their memories. They're delicious, you should try it sometime."

Macey gasped. "You're eating people's memories?"

"Have you not felt confused after exiting the Staran?"

"Yes, but I thought that was normal..."

The voice inside her mind gaggled. "It is normal, ever since I moved in. It's been a long time, and my appetite has grown. So has that of my brothers and sisters. I believe you have met one of them. He doesn't enjoy memories though; his taste is a little different."

"You don't mean the Voice? You can't, no. He's not like you, he's real."

"Who's saying I'm not real? Just because I'm talking to you in your head doesn't mean I don't exist outside of it. I'm only using the dark side of your mind as a host, nothing more, nothing less. I'm giving it a body, just like my brother personifies the Mahoun. The devil. He's a dramatic one, he had to choose the evilest person known to humans."

Macey was having a hard time keeping up. "So, he isn't the devil, he's just impersonating him?"

"Silly Macey. There is no devil, but as long as people believe in one, there's an empty space to be filled. A vacuum that aches for a host. So, my brother took it for himself, taking on some of its perceived traits and looks. It's why he doesn't go outside much. The devil is too hideous to be seen, and he's a vain one."

"How many of you are there?"

The voice - her voice - laughed. "Now that would be telling. I'm not going to endanger my siblings just to satisfy your curiosity. It's time for you to give up."

"Wait, if your brother personifies the devil, whose shape do you take?"

"Haven't you figured it out yet? I'm Self-Doubt. I'm the evil little voice inside everyone's head. And believe me, everybody has it. Especially people travelling through the Staran. People who are travelling always have doubts. *Am I going in the right direction? Did I forget something? Am I making the right decision? Should I have brought my sword? Will the journey hurt?* You get the picture."

Macey was beginning to wonder why sludge-Macey... Self-Doubt was still talking to her. Why would it freely give up all this information? It didn't seem difficult enough. Unless it was trying to distract her from something important.

She'd learned enough for now. What she really needed to focus on was getting out of the Staran and taking the black blob with her. Then she could go back to the other Wardens and make plans on how to get rid of the other impersonators. Starting with the Voice. And maybe she could celebrate her success with some alone time with her men. She'd not even kissed them properly since they'd been reunited. She missed their touch.

There she was, getting distracted again. Focus, Macey.

She needed to get out of here. But why was thinking getting so difficult? And breathing? Why wasn't she breathing?

Something had to be wrong in the real world.

"Finally figuring it out?" Self-Doubt was whispering. "It may be too late for you."

Panicked, Macey looked around. How did she get out of the Staran? She took a step back, but once again bumped into the barrier. She carefully walked forwards, her arms outstretched. She didn't want to crash into an invisible wall for a second time.

Not far from where the black circle had been on the floor, she found the barrier. So, she couldn't go back into the direction she'd come from either.

Trapped.

Not enough air.

"Nobody has ever died in here before," the voice in her mind said cheerily. "I'm going to enjoy the experience."

"No, you're not," Macey growled. "I'm getting out of here."

But she wasn't all that confident anymore. Black spots were beginning to dance in front of her eyes. Less and less oxygen reached her lungs which were screaming for air.

Air.

Air!

She sent out a cry for help, hoping that her seventh Warden would hear it. All she needed was some air to breathe so she could concentrate and think. Then she'd figure out a way to get out of this place. And to defeat Self-Doubt.

Was this what drowning felt like? If so, she felt particularly sorry for all the sailors in tales of old who died at sea.

And no wonder people hated kelpies, if this is what they were rumoured to do to people.

The black spots intensified, and she clutched at her throat, clawing it with her nails.

Shift.

She needed to shift.

The thought fled the moment she had it, and she struggled to pull it back.

How had she forgotten how to shift? That shouldn't be possible, should it?

Why hadn't her body taken over the moment she hit the water?

Where was her natural instinct?

The panic grew worse with each unanswered question, and her vision swam all the more.

Another moment passed, and she did the only thing she could think of. She opened her mouth and gulped down the water which was suddenly surrounding her.

Selkie

16

Water spurted from Macey's mouth as coughs wracked her entire body.

Wait...coughs? That meant...

She opened her eyes and blinked furiously. The sting of the salt water making them ache and urging her to rub them. She just about refrained, knowing it would only make them worse, and not better.

"You're lucky to be alive, kelpie," a haunting male voice said.

She flipped over onto her back, trying to ignore the fact she was naked and there was a man in front of her.

While her vision was still swimming, she could just about make out the silhouette of a short, lithe man with what could probably only be described as a swimmer's body, standing over her.

He was naked too.

Macey blinked again, trying to make sense of what she was seeing. What were the chances of the person who saved her being naked too?

"Who are you?" Macey croaked, her voice a mere echo of its normal strength. She wouldn't even have recognised it as her own. Well, other than the fact she was the one speaking.

She briefly wondered if Self-Doubt was still with her, but from the lack of persistent taunting in her head, she guessed that the answer was no. Hopefully it would stay away, though she knew she'd probably have to face it again.

At least they knew what it was that was destroying the Staran now. That piece of knowledge was going to be invaluable going forward.

"I'm Rónán," he replied.

Macey sat up suddenly. "You're a selkie."

"Last I checked. Unfortunately, my mother was rather inventive in naming me, so I got stuck with a name that screams what I am to the world." He chuckled slightly.

"Why did you help me?" she asked, her head swimming slightly from the effects of a lack of air.

"Why wouldn't I? Just because there are rumours of your people, doesn't mean I have to believe them. In fact, I think it gives me more reasons to ignore them. After all, don't your people have the same tales about mine?"

"Yes, I believe so," Macey answered, her voice still rough and achy. "But, if I'm honest, I'd have expected those rumours to be a big enough influence to stop any selkies from helping me."

"Maybe it would have, for some of the younger ones. Especially those influenced by the old ways. But my herd isn't the kind to take those things seriously. And we never have been. Plus, I didn't know you were a kelpie until I got you onto land. And what were my options then? Re-drown you?"

"So, I did actually drown?" Macey attempted to clarify.

"I believe so, yes. That's normally what happens when you open your human mouth under water," he said, clearly unimpressed.

"I had no choice," she pointed out, knowing it was true, but not knowing how she could convince anyone else of that.

"I didn't think you did. Otherwise it's a rather silly thing to do unless you're heartbroken."

"No, definitely not that," she replied. "Are there any others about?" she asked nervously, thinking of how he'd mentioned that his herd weren't bothered by the rumours about kelpies, but some of the others might be.

If one of those others was about, then she could be in serious trouble.

"Not that I'm aware of, I didn't sense anyone else out in the water, and I'm normally able to. But don't worry, if you're under my protection, then most selkies will leave you alone anyway. Unless they're trying to prove something."

"Reassuring," Macey answered.

"Isn't it just."

They lapsed into silence for a moment. Macey wasn't sure quite what to say to the man. Except...

"Thank you for saving me," she croaked.

"You're very welcome. I'm not in the habit of letting anyone drown."

"That's good to know," she replied.

Slowly, she climbed to her feet, wobbling slightly as she reached them. Whatever had happened down there had severely weakened her human body. And it hadn't been in the best of shapes to start with. Exhausted and malnourished were more the terms that came to mind when she considered her health. Hopefully, after they healed the Staran here, they'd be able to rest.

She turned around, and looked back inland, trying to work out whereabouts on the island she was, and how she could get back to her men, but coming up with nothing. She really should have studied the maps closer.

Then again, she hadn't planned to become stranded on one of the coasts.

The selkie coughed. "Are you aware you have six marks on your back?" he asked.

"Ye...six?" She spun around to face him. "Did you say six?"

"Yes, there's six. Five smaller ones in an almost circle, with the sixth larger in the middle. There appears to be a gap though."

"Six..." she repeated, realising that must have meant she'd gained her own mark. Just Izban's left to collect then. That was a start, even if she wasn't aware of just how to actually manage that.

Then again, this whole adventure had been a mystery from start to finish. She didn't see why now would be any different.

"Do you know where we are?" she asked the selkie.

"Of course," Rónán replied.

"How far is it to Village Bay?"

"Maybe fifteen minutes' walk? Are you cold, by the way?"

She blushed a little, reminded that both of them were still naked. She hoped her men wouldn't see her like that, they might get jealous. Waves, she'd get jealous if she saw them naked with another girl.

"I'm fine, but I need to get there quickly. Just point me in the direction and I'm sure I'll find it."

He frowned. "Trying to get rid of me?"

"Not at all, but don't you have better things to do?"

Rónán chuckled. "Now that I saved you, I'd quite like to know you're continuing to be safe. Do you have friends here on the island?"

Macey nodded. "Yes, several of them. We're only here to do... a task. Something I tried to do and almost drowned. We'll leave as soon as we're done with that."

"Pity, it's rare that we get visitors here who aren't humans. There's been too many tourists recently that we have to hide from. And divers, exploring the sea caves. There were none today though, so I took the chance to go for a dive in my favourite cave - that's where I found you. Were you exploring them as well?"

"Something like that," Macey muttered, but then had an idea. "Have you ever noticed the crystal in that cave? On the pedestal?"

"Of course. It's been there as long as I can remember. Generations of selkies have tried to lift if off its stand, but none have succeeded. It's become a bit of a tradition for young selkies to try, like King Arthur's sword. Why are you asking?"

"Just wondering, it looked so pretty," Macey evaded the question. "But shall we walk back to the village? I may be getting a little cold after all."

HER MEN SPOTTED her before Macey could see them. They ran up the hill the kelpie and the selkie were descending from and before she knew it, Macey was wrapped in Flint's warm arms.

"You're freezing. Here, let me warm you."

Hot air enveloped Macey and her goosebumps slowly disappeared. She hugged Flint back, reveling in his touch and warmth. Right now, the Fire Warden was exactly what she needed.

"Who are you?" Cam asked Rónán with barely hidden hostility. The selkie was standing behind Macey, looking a little uncomfortable. Not because of his nakedness, but because the three men were glaring at him.

"I'm the selkie who saved your girlfriend's life."

That shut up Cam and Macey was glad about it. She didn't need them start a testosterone-induced fight.

"What happened?" Flint asked Macey, still holding her tight in his arms.

"I underestimated the thing inside the Staran. But I know now why they're dying, and I know more about the Voice too. How about we return to the house and talk about it there? I'd love to put on some clothes too."

"Don't worry, I brought them with me," Jared said

cheerily and produced the clothes Macey had shed before she'd shifted earlier. She quickly put them on, but handed her jacket to Rónán.

"You can bind it around your waist," she suggested. "You don't want to give Amber and Izban a heart attack."

Rónán laughed but did as she'd suggested. "Who are those two? Prudes?"

"No, but Amber is the youngest of us," Macey said. "It seems that I'm a bit protective of her virtue."

Jared laughed. "You don't want to know what they were doing when we came to look for you. I don't think there's much left of her virtue."

Macey cringed. "Stop it, I don't want to imagine them snogging."

"Didn't you encourage them to work out their sexual tension not long ago?"

"Yes, but..." Macey shook her head. She didn't know why she was suddenly thinking of Amber in that protective way. Like a big sister, even though there were only a few years between them.

"Let's go back," Cam suggested. "I can't wait to hear what's been going on in the cave and why you suddenly brought a selkie along. I thought your two kinds didn't get on."

Rónán and Macey sighed in unison.

"That animosity is based on a lot of nasty

rumours on both sides," Rónán explained. "But the two of us seem to be mostly unaffected by those."

Macey cringed a little, remembering how anti-selkie she'd been in the past. She'd certainly become more tolerant in recent weeks, mainly because she'd not had any exposure to other kinds of supernaturals before. Now she was surrounded by them and she loved the variety.

It turned out they were only a few minutes away from Luch's house, but despite the short distance, Macey wished she was wearing shoes. The ground was full of pointy stones that hurt her bare feet. She almost debated a partial shift so she could have her webbed hooves, but that seemed too much of an effort. With all the adrenaline caused by almost drowning, she'd forgotten how tired she was, but now that she was safe with her men, the exhaustion returned.

"Macey!" Amber was standing in the doorway, waving as she saw them approach. "We were worried about you!"

"Everything's fine!" she called back. "More or less," she added under her breath. She was going to need some tea to get the strength to explain everything.

. . .

A FEW MINUTES LATER, she was wrapped in a blanket and had her hands curled around a warm mug of tea. Flint had dried her hair, although he'd managed to make it extraordinarily frizzy. Rónán had been given the same treatment - except for the hair. His short blond hair had been dried by the wind already.

Taking a long sip of tea to strengthen herself, Macey told the other Wardens about what had occured down in the sea cave. Somehow, she didn't mind Rónán hearing it all. It wasn't as if it was a secret, and if he wanted to stay along and be confused by her strange tale, that was fine. She liked the selkie, even though she'd only met him half an hour ago. She had a good feeling about him; maybe he'd be one of their future allies. They could certainly use having the selkies on their side. There were a lot of them, many more than kelpies.

"So, this thing inside the Staran is the same as the Voice?" Izban asked, summarising what Macey had told them.

"Yes, and it said that there are many more of them. If they can take on different shapes and purposes, they're going to be hard to find. I did see a tiny connection reaching out from this one though, so if we somehow managed to follow that, we'd be able to find them one by one. Maybe you have a spell for that?"

Izban nodded. "Possibly. I'd need to look at it first."

"I might be able to help with that," Jared said, making them all look at the incubus. "You said there was a hole in the cave ceiling that let in light and air, right?"

"Yes, it was tiny though."

"Then you're lucky I'm Earth," Jared replied with a grin. "If we find that hole, I can get us all down there. Maybe together we'll be able to kill that Self-Doubt thing and heal the Staran - at least for now."

"If you don't mind, Bradaigh and I will stay here," Luch said with a cheeky smile. "We have some catching up to do."

Macey smiled back. "Of course. Now that all seven of us are united, it should be doable. This will be our first big test. Time to show the world that we really are the Wardens."

She just hoped that overconfidence wasn't yet another sibling of Self-Doubt.

With Rónán's help, it didn't take them long to find the hole. It was covered almost completely by bushes of sorrel, but thanks to Jared's Earth magic, he was able to spot it despite the plants.

"Clever, it almost looks like a puffin burrow," Cam remarked. "The perfect camouflage."

To Macey's disappointment, they'd not spotted any puffins yet. Maybe it was the wrong season. She loved those tiny, comical birds, even though she'd only seen them once before. But the grassy slope they were standing on was covered in burrows where they'd lay their eggs in the summer.

"The cave ceiling was stone, right, not earth?" Jared asked Macey and she nodded.

"Yes, beautiful smooth stone. No stalactites, strangely enough."

"Good, that will make it easier to find where the earth ends and the cave begins. You may all want to step back a little."

They did as he asked, watching curiously as he kneeled on the ground and put his hands on the wet grass. He closed his eyes and seemed to concentrate hard.

The ground began to rumble and shake, but it was only a gentle tremor, nothing as bad as what Macey had experienced down below in the cave. She was a little sad that she wasn't diving into it this time. It had been so beautiful to see the world beneath St Kilda, but she understood that the others had to take the boring route.

Scratch that. Clumps of earth were floating into the air as Jared furrowed his brow. They hung above the ground while the hole slowly expanded.

Macey hadn't seen Jared's magic in action yet, but somehow, she hadn't imagined it to be this strong and impressive. Tiny beads of sweat were beginning to form on his forehead as he heaved more and more earth into the air. She watched with bated breath as the hole turned into a shaft wide enough to fit even someone Flint's size through.

Finally, Jared let out a sigh of exhaustion and the balls of earth fell to the ground, far away from the hole they once covered.

"How do we get down there?" Rónán asked but Macey shook her head.

"I'm not sure you should come with us. I think this is a Warden thing that we have to do ourselves."

"I could stand guard, in case you drown yourself again?"

Macey cringed. Maybe it was a good idea after all to have another person with them who wasn't directly involved.

"Okay," she admitted. "But try and keep back, no matter what happens once we touch the crystal."

The selkie nodded. "Of course. But again, how do we get down there? I don't fancy jumping."

Cam laughed. "Wind Warden, at your service. Who'd like to be first?"

When nobody volunteered, Macey sighed and stepped forward. "I trust you," she told him with a smile. But please don't let me fall nonetheless."

He chuckled. "Stand by the hole and keep your arms close to your body. Call when you're at the bottom, then I'll send the next person down."

She did as he'd asked. Before she could even say something, she was gently lifted into the air. It was strange; she couldn't feel anything holding her, not even something beneath her feet. She'd expected an air cushion or something like that to stand on, but no, it was as if she was floating weightlessly. It was a strange feeling and she wasn't quite sure if she liked it.

She hovered over to her right until she was straight above the hole. She refused to look down. Not that she was suffering from vertigo, but she didn't want to tempt it either.

Slowly, she sank down into the earth, descending through the dark tunnel Jared had created. It was wide enough that she could have reached out to touch the walls, but she kept Cam's warning in mind and resisted the temptation.

She only looked down once the shaft widened and she entered the cave.

It looked just like it had earlier that day, except that there was slightly less water surrounding the pedestal. The tide had to be out, which was a good omen. No drowning this time, hopefully. Flint would feel more comfortable soon, being surrounded by more air than water. She really didn't understand his aversion to water. Sure, it was the opposite element of fire, but her element was water and she didn't feel uncomfortable around fire.

When she landed softly on the stone slab the pedestal stood on, she called for Cam to lower the next one down into the cave.

Amber arrived with a smile on her face. "It's strange to fly without flying," she said to Macey as they waited for the others. "I think I enjoyed it."

Izban didn't look as happy as her, and neither did Jared. Flint had some trouble squeezing through the final bit of the shaft, but he didn't seem to mind his shirt being a little muddy. Rónán whooped as he was lowered down by Cam, obviously not used to such magic. Macey was wondering whether selkies had any magic of their own, besides the ability to shift into seals. She was going to have to ask him later, once their task was done.

Cam himself flew down fast, almost falling, only stopping when he was inches away from hitting the ground.

They all assembled around the pedestal. The stone slab below was just big enough to let them stand on it without getting wet feet. As promised, Rónán stayed back a little, letting the Wardens form a circle around the crystal. It looked just as it had before: beautiful and glistening in the light coming through the hole in the ceiling.

"I'm not sure what is going to happen once we all touch it," Macey warned as she put her hands on the crystal. "Maybe we'll all be in the same place, maybe we'll each have to fight Self-Doubt on our own. Don't forget that you're strong. We all are. We don't have any reason to doubt ourselves. There's a reason we were chosen as Wardens, so let's prove that we can defeat this evil thing."

"Well said," Cam smiled and placed his hands next

to Macey's. "Let's show that if you mess with one of us, you will feel the wrath of all seven Wardens."

The others didn't seem interested in doing heroic speeches, and simply touched the crystal.

"What now?" Jared asked, but a second later, Macey was pulled by her navel and pushed into darkness.

SEVEN STONE THRONES... she knew this place! Macey got up from the floor where she had landed and looked around for the others. All of them were here, by her side, either on the ground or in the process of getting up while swaying slightly. Izban seemed close to throwing up.

"Is this the place you were dreaming of?" Amber asked in wonder, walking to the nearest stone throne and running a finger over the smooth surface.

"Yes, but back then, there were people here."

This time, the thrones were empty. They were alone.

"Do you think we need to sit on them?" Flint asked, walking to the one next to Amber's.

Macey shrugged. "I don't see why not. Maybe something will happen then? This isn't what I experienced earlier. It was all very different then, shinier and less dark. No room but a tunnel. Well, it wasn't at all like this."

"I'll take the biggest one," Jared shouted and ran over to the one furthest away from where they had landed. Macey laughed when she saw his enthusiasm. It was good to have some humour in this strange place.

She took one on Amber's right. It was made from black marble, the dark stone interlaced with silver-grey strands. She hesitantly sat down on it, but in the end, it was just a chair. A very fancy, stone chair that was in a throne room. She ignored that bit, it was too strange.

Hadn't the former Warden in her vision said that one day, this throne room would appear for them all? She just hadn't expected it to be this soon. And why did they need thrones?

Cam was the last to sit down, looking down at his seat in bewilderment. "It says Camdan on the head-rest," he told the others. "But it appeared out of nowhere."

Macey turned around, looking at her own back-rest. True, her name was suddenly engraved in a golden, swirly font. How very weird.

"My name is here, too," Amber confirmed.

"And mine," Izban added. "What does it mean?"

"I think these thrones are now permanently

ours," Macey said slowly. "Maybe we've taken over from the previous Wardens officially?"

"Yes, you have," a new, sad voice suddenly said. Luch.

The woman appeared out of thin air in the centre of the throne room, first translucent, then slowly becoming more flesh and blood until she looked fully human.

"Luch? What are you doing here?" Izban asked sharply. "What's going on?"

He sounded slightly panicked, which was exactly what Macey was experiencing. She had a bad feeling about this.

"A new beginning means the ending of something old," Luch replied, her voice missing its usual spark. "To have the full power of the Wardens, which you need to defeat this evil, it needs to be taken from the last ones. And the very first."

"No way!" Macey shouted, jumping up from her throne. "You've co-existed with the other sets of Wardens, just continue doing that. We don't mind!"

"It's time that I join my husband on the other side. He's had to wait for me for far too long. And now that I've got to meet the six of you, I know that the Wardens' legacy is in safe hands." She smiled again, but it couldn't hide her sadness. "Please make it worth it. Defeat the parasite clinging onto the Staran, defeat Mahoun, defeat all of these evil beings affecting the world. Although with the first one, Self-Doubt, I may still be able to help you."

"Is there no other way?" Amber asked, tears making her eyes look large and bright.

"No, little beithir, there isn't. So don't cry. I've lived a long time and I've not been able to touch my husband for most of it. You should be happy for me."

A tear ran down Macey's cheek. "Then why are you so sad?" she asked Luch, who looked at her in surprise.

"I'm not sad about my death. I'm sad to leave you alone, without my help." She stood up tall, turning around until she'd looked at every Warden. "Are you ready to take your first big step as the Seven Wardens? Are you ready to make a decision over life and death?"

Despite her tears, Macey nodded and saw that the others did the same. They were united in grief for a woman they hardly knew, but who was going to sacrifice herself for the future of this world.

"Luch... thank you," Macey whispered, her voice breaking.

The woman smiled. "You're very welcome. Now, on to business. I'm going to summon Self-Doubt and will try to fight it. It will see me as the most delicious meal it's ever seen. I have a long life of memories for it to feed from, so hopefully, it'll be distracted. Kill it while it's not paying you any attention."

"How do we do that?" Cam asked. "From what Macey said, that thing didn't have a real shape while it was in the Staran, just a blob."

Luch grimaced. "It will take on my form. A sludge-Luch, as Macey would call it." She gave the kelpie a wink. "While it's in that shape, you will be able to kill it like you would any other being. But be quick before it notices and changes back."

"Magic or physical power?" Flint asked, stretching his arms so his strong muscles showed.

Luch tsked. "Why do you think the Wardens aren't human this time? Any human could run a knife through me. No, it has to be magic. As we don't know what will affect it the most, how about you all fire whatever you have at it?"

"But what if we hit you?" Amber asked, worry creasing her face.

"Then you hit me," Luch replied calmly. "I'm going to die today no matter what. At least if it's lightning, it will be over quick. Don't worry about me. Worry about being fast so you can kill Self-Doubt before it becomes immaterial again."

"We'll make you proud," Jared announced, surprising Macey. She hadn't realised he was attached to Luch. Maybe their time waiting together outside the sìth queendom had turned them into friends without her noticing.

"Good. Are you ready?"

Macey summoned some water and wrapped it around her wrists, ready to throw it at her enemy. Lightning began to flash around Amber, while flames licked at Flint's fingers. A tiny whirlwind formed on Cam's side and both Izban and Jared stretched out their hands towards the centre of the room where Luch was standing, proud and calm.

"Thank you, Luch," Macey said once again. "We're ready."

The woman nodded and sat down on the floor, cross-legged as if she was meditating. She closed her eyes while the Wardens looked at her, everyone ready to strike at a moment's notice.

A dark mist began to rise from the ground where Luch sat, enveloping her slowly. What started as grey wafts became thick fog, and Macey was wondering if it would stay that way. They'd have no chance attacking mist. There was nothing to focus their magic on.

Luckily, the fog thickened even further until it formed a shape. Moments later, a second Luch was sitting on the floor, facing the real one. Just like sludge-Macey, Luch's doppelganger was black without detailed features and seemed to be made from tar or black oil. It leaned over to Luch as if it was sniffing the air, before stretching out a hand to touch the woman. Luch was keeping her eyes closed and Macey knew she would have done the same. It was one thing looking death into the eye, but quite another to see yourself about to kill you.

She tightened her grip on her magic. This was their only chance to kill Self-Doubt. It had to work.

Macey did a quick survey of the others. They were all ready and looking at her. She took a deep breath and nodded, giving the signal to strike.

What followed next was chaos. Lightning, water, fire, wind and ice flew at Luch and her clone, meeting in one giant explosion of light. Macey was thrown back by the shock wave, but luckily, she'd been standing in front of her throne and was now slumped on the seat. She got back up as fast as she could and threw more water into the middle of the room. She couldn't see Luch anymore, there was too much magic happening around her. The ground was rumbling and suddenly, sharp shards of earth flew at the point where Luch had been sitting. They looked as piercing as spears and were surely able to kill a human. But was it all enough to kill the evil that had copied Luch?

She formed a giant ball of water and had it hover above the centre of the room.

"Amber!" she shouted. "Give me some lightning!"

The beithir immediately grasped what Macey was planning and nodded. "Three... two... one... now!"

Lightning crashed into the water at the same time

as Macey released it. Sparks flew and hot steam rose to the ceiling.

A sharp scream came from their target, but it wasn't Luch's voice. It was someone else, someone in a lot of pain. Hopefully, it was the sound of Self-Doubt dying.

"Again!" Macey shouted and conjured another ball of water. "Now!"

Even quicker than before, Amber's lightning entered the water, and more steam filled the room.

The cries disappeared, but the Wardens continued to throw their elements at it. They were taking no chances. Macey dared a quick glance around. Flint was covered in soot but seemed elated at being able to create so much fire. Cam was breathing heavily, sending whirlwinds towards Flint who infused them with fire before Cam directed them into the middle of the room. Izban was throwing icicles while Jared threw similarly shaped earth lances.

Everyone was giving all they could. Was it enough?

When Macey tried to create yet another water ball and failed to even get a drop of water, she knew they had to stop. They'd be defenseless if the evil being wasn't dead yet.

"Stop!" she shouted as loud as she could and immediately, the others ceased their attack. It took a moment for the smoke and dust to clear. Carefully, Macey approached the place where Luch had been sitting.

There was nothing left of the woman and her doppelganger but a pile of ashes, one of them white, one dark.

She sank to her knees, grief overwhelming her. She'd not met Luch long ago, and yet she felt as if they'd known each other for a long time. Maybe it was because Luch had been a Warden like herself. Maybe they were kindred spirits.

Amber kneeled down by Macey's side, her tears flowing freely.

"Thank you, Luch," the beithir whispered. "Rest in peace."

She was weary to the bone, and hardly wanted to move at all, but that wasn't going to stop her on her mission. Not when she finally had time where she didn't need to be anywhere, or defeating anything, and with all three of her men in one room.

Oh, the things she could do with them all in one room. If they could see her thoughts, she was sure even Jared would blush.

Flint closed the door, and turned the lock, effectively shutting them in for the night. Macey wasn't going to complain. She couldn't think of a better place to be.

After checking that all three sets of eyes were on her, Macey untied the robe she was wearing with fumbling fingers and dropped it to the floor. Even though she'd already been naked today, she felt suddenly slightly self-conscious. Maybe because it had been months since she'd been with any of her men. Even if it didn't feel like that at times. She really had lost track of time while being trapped in the Voice's Keep.

"Macey..." Flint warned.

"Yes?" she asked as innocently as she could, looking up at him with an expression that would leave no doubt what her intentions were.

"Didn't you hear what Amber said, you need rest," he attempted, but his voice cracked at the end, and his eyes strayed, leaving no doubt that he'd be easy to persuade.

"Of course I did. But some things are a little more important than rest right now."

She sashayed up to him, swaying her hips slightly and could feel Jared and Cam watching her.

Rising on her tiptoes, her mouth came close to Flint's ear. "And just think how well I'll sleep once I'm completely spent," she whispered.

A low moan came from Flint's throat, and, without warning, he scooped her up into his arms.

Macey let out a small squeal, but it wasn't anything for her to worry about.

Flint marched them over to the bed, before dropping her on to it. She squealed again as she bounced slightly on the mattress. But she didn't care, hopefully it would make it clear to her men just how much she wanted them.

Jared moved in, once Flint had backed away a little, and smothered her body under his as he leaned down to kiss her.

It started out sweet, a gentle brush of his lips against hers. But Macey wasn't having any of that.

She ran her tongue over his bottom lip, making Jared chuckle into their kiss before pulling back slightly. "Eager, are we?"

"Yes," she said breathlessly, needing him closer.

She reached down between them, relieved her men were already naked, and making access that bit easier for her. She took his cock in her hand, and began to stroke it up and down, going as slowly as she dared.

"Macey," Jared groaned. "You're not going to be able to do that for long."

"You are playing with fire a little bit," Cam chuckled, sounding close already.

She was relieved. All three of them had been further away than she'd have liked.

"Wouldn't that be if I was touching Flint?" she asked innocently.

"Don't tempt me, Macey. It can be arranged," her Fire Warden answered.

She whimpered. "Arrange it," she said, not regretting her words in the slightest.

"As you wish," he replied.

Jared moved off her, and cold air hit her skin. Not that it mattered, she was hot in *all* the right places. It'd take nothing short of an ice bath to cool her down. Especially with all the anticipation building within her.

"Please," she begged, hoping one of them would do something, and fast.

"Turn over," Jared said, trailing a hand over her stomach and making her arch into his touch. She wanted more of it. More of them.

So, she did exactly what he said.

"On your hands and knees, please," he asked, smoothing his hand over her back, leaving a trail of goosebumps in his wake. She hoped he touched her more firmly next time. So she could actually *feel* him against her skin, and not just the tease of his fingertips against her.

That was just going to drive her crazy.

Once she'd done that, Flint leaned down and kissed her firmly, slipping his tongue into her mouth, and using it to caress her own.

"You need to tell us if something we do isn't okay," he whispered once he'd pulled back slightly. "None of us want you to feel uncomfortable."

Macey nodded, then kissed him again, deepening it the moment she could. Now wasn't the time for words, it was time for actions on all their parts.

Jared's second hand joined his first, and she arched upwards into his touch, probably looking a little like a cat stretching. But she was beyond caring. She didn't mind how she looked, so long as they kept their hands and lips on her.

"Eager, aren't we?" Jared chuckled.

"It's been a long time," Macey moaned, breaking her kiss with Flint.

She looked up at him, barely able to focus as Jared's hands strayed lower and began to caress her ass. She pushed back into him, her every movement involuntary.

Not that she minded. Her body could do what she liked so long as it brought her men closer to her.

Preferably as close as they could possibly get. In her, surrounding her, consuming her.

"Please," she begged, not too sure what she was asking for.

"As you wish," Jared replied, his hands leaving her.

Macey whimpered, wanting them back against her right away. She wasn't left to wonder about what he was doing for long, as his hot breath came against the inside of her thigh, causing anticipation to build inside her. This was far beyond what she could have imagined or asked for. Especially knowing that Cam and Flint were watching. Hopefully, they'd be doing more than that soon.

She thought about begging again, but decided against it. There wasn't going to be anything that stopped them now. Not with the door locked, and everything sorted for now. They were safe. Or as safe as they were going to be while the world was still in danger.

Jared kissed the inside of her thigh, making her whimper slightly.

When he moved higher still, her whimper transformed into a moan, and she pushed back into him, eager for him to pay her more attention.

"Look here, Macey," Flint said, his own voice dripping with need.

It was only then she'd noticed she'd hung her head as a result of Jared's teasing.

She looked up, to find Flint's hooded eyes boring into her, his hand on his cock, stroking slowly as he watched her slightly parted lips.

Macey's tongue darted out and Flint's breath hitched as he took in the sight. She hoped he'd take it as the invitation it was. She watched eagerly as his hand left his cock, only for him to stroke her hair with it. She leaned into his touch, closing her eyes as she did.

It may make her feel wanton to be naked in a bed with three men, but there was far more to it. She may have said the words mostly to appease Self-Doubt, but she really did believe the connection between them was real. It was something deep down within them all.

And she could feel it stronger than ever right now.

Jared took the opportunity to finally reach the destination she wanted him too, drawing his tongue along her gently, but still only teasing. She gave off a soft whimper, making Flint chuckle.

"Don't worry, he's not going to stop," he said, moving his hand under Macey's chin and tipping it upwards. "But will you?"

Macey shook her head as more whimpers escaped. Jared hooked his arms around her thighs and pulled her back into him, just as Flint presented Macey with his cock.

She didn't need telling twice, and took him into her mouth, trying to focus on what was happening, even as Jared increased the pressure down below.

The angle she was at had Flint's cock touching the back of her throat and she was struggling not to gag. But she didn't want to stop, something he seemed to pick up from how she ran her tongue along the underside of him.

Flint's hands tangled in her hair as he began to thrust gently in and out of her mouth. She did her best to keep her teeth to herself, not wanting to hurt him. But Flint didn't seem to care. His thrusts were becoming more and more erratic as he got closer to finishing.

She might just end up falling over the edge.

Jared had moved his attentions to her clit, circling it with his tongue and causing her to buck backwards into him. He chuckled, the vibrations only heightening the sensations crashing through her.

All she needed now was...

That.

Cam's hands began to caress the skin of her back. It almost felt as if he was tracing each of the marks she had there with his fingers. But she couldn't focus enough to be able to tell.

Not that it would help. She actually had no idea what they all looked like. At some point, she'd have to get someone to draw a picture of them. He continued his exploration, going as far as grabbing her ass, but not far enough to slip a finger inside her. Though she wanted that more than anything.

She couldn't really ask for it while she had a mouthful of Flint though. She renewed her attentions on him, rubbing her tongue along the underside of his cock, and using her lips to suck on him.

Flint gasped and grasped her hair tighter.

"I think she wants it," he managed to grind out through his teeth.

Macey wasn't sure what silent communication passed between her men, but Jared left his position behind her, and she felt somewhat bereft. At least, until he re-positioned himself underneath her, and gently resumed his attentions, lapping his tongue against her sensitive skin.

It was Cam who surprised her, running his hands up and down her back, before one slipped between her legs.

Macey shuddered in anticipation. There was no doubt in her mind about what was going to happen next, and she welcomed it. She just wasn't too sure how to encourage it.

"Hold still, Macey," Flint said, holding her head steady, and stroking her hair. He knew what was going to come too and was trying to make it as easy as possible for her. She appreciated it. But equally, she wished Cam would get on with it. She'd gone too long without feeling one of her men inside her.

Jared's hands travelled upwards, ad he continued to twirl his tongue around her clit. The only thing that had stopped her from exploding already was wanting to wait for Cam and concentrating on the attention she was giving Flint.

But when Jared pinched her nipples, she gave a short shriek, the sound muffled slightly by Flint's cock, but she was sure it was unmistakable to them.

Cam chose that moment to slip a finger inside her.

"Oh, Macey," he said, chuckling along as he did. "You're enjoying this."

She nodded carefully.

"Well then, it'd be cruel to keep you from what you want," he teased.

He withdrew his finger, using it to tease her by drawing it around her entrance.

She wanted to beg again. To ask him to take her, so all three of them were touching her. All three of them were hers.

Luckily, Cam didn't wait much longer, and without hesitation, thrust into her.

It was almost too much. With Cam filling her, and Flint resuming his slow pace thrusting in and out of her mouth, she was almost lost already. But Jared's tongue against her clit, and his fingers pinching her nipples, were causing things to tighten deep within her.

Her whole body was lost, and she knew she wouldn't be able to hold any thoughts in her mind except those about how perfectly her men fit her.

She briefly wondered whether Jared was getting enough to top up his incubus nature from this, but he chose that exact moment to twist one of her nipples. Macey cried out around Flint's cock, spurring all three of them on.

The pace increased and became almost frantic from them all. The room was filled with the sound of skin against skin, and the scent of sex. There was no doubt this was how things were supposed to be.

Macey's head began to spin, though not in an unpleasant way, and her body began to shake slightly. She wasn't going to be able to last much longer.

Judging from Flint's ragged breathing, he wasn't going to last much longer either.

"You can let go, Macey," Cam said, his voice broken by the ragged breathing, as his pace became frantic inside her.

It was too much for Macey to take. Everything was just too much.

Her vision began to fade, and her arms and legs started to buckle as she lost control of keeping herself upright. Luckily, her men had her, and held her tightly, keeping up the pressure inside her. While slightly uncomfortable, it would only make things better.

Like a tidal wave, it became too much, and the release crashed over her, causing her to shudder and shake. She was dimly aware of Flint moving away from her, and of Cam thrusting into her one final time and finding his own release.

Besides, none of that mattered. The only thing that did was the bliss washing over her.

She collapsed down onto the bed once the feeling receded. Spent, and satisfied with her men tangled up beside her. She might still need to save the world, but for the moment, she was content.

Macey's eyes fluttered closed. She couldn't have kept them open if she'd tried. But she knew that was alright. She had her men with her. She had her allies by her side. Their problems could wait for a night. Maybe even for a day or two. But she needed this. She needed the time to reset herself.

Then they'd continue the fight.

Then they could actually save the world.

At least, Macey hoped they could.

~ The End ~

Wait, what's going on with Nessie? Will they be able to finish their quest? Is Rónán really as hot as he sounds? Find out in the next book in the Seven Wardens series, Beneath the Earth.

And if you want to find out more about Amber and Izban's story and how they met, then take a look at Through the Storms.

Subscribe to our newsletters for all the latest books:
Skye: skyemackinnon.com/newsletter
Laura: www.authorlauragreenwood.co.uk/p/mailing-list-sign-up.html

GLOSSARY

Adlet - Inuit descendent of a dog & human

Almas - Mongolian humanoid creature

Angakok - Inuit priest/shaman

Aos Sìth - Fairy Folk

Atliarusek - Inuit gnome sized man

Baobhan Sìth - Incubus

Beithir - Venomous Reptile, a cross between a snake and a dragon

Caladrius - a snow white bird that lives in the house of a King and can heal illness and injury

Cat Sìth - Cat Shifters

Ceasg - A mermaid with a salmon tail who can grant wishes

Cù Sìth - Dog Shifters

Daimon - Guiding Spirit (Greek)

Fàth-Fiata - Magic Fog/Mist

Fedelm - Irish Celtic Prophet

Gashadokuro - Giant Japanese skeletons that bite off heads and drink blood

Kabouter - Flemish Gnomes

Kelpie - Mythical water horse

Kludde - Flemish Shapeshifter and Trickster

Lampad - Nymphs of the Underworld who bear torches. Their light can send travelers mad

Loch - Scottish word for lake

Luch - Gaelic word for mouse

Maniilaq - Inuit 19th Century prophet

Merry Dancer - Descended from fallen angels, they now make up the northern lights

Mongolian Death Worm - underground worm

Seachd-sìona - Seven Elements

Meer - Flemish for Lake

Na Fir Gorma - Storm Kelpies/Blue Men of Minch

Seelie - Light fae folk

Selkie - Man or woman who can clothe themselves in seal skin

Sìth - Faerie/Fae

Staran - Gaelic for path

Tornak - Inuit Guardian Soul

Unseelie - Dark fae folk

Watershee - A fairy like being who often acts like a siren

ABOUT SKYE MACKINNON

Skye MacKinnon is a USA Today & International Bestselling Author whose books are filled with strong heroines who don't have to choose.

She embraces her Scottishness with fantastical Scottish settings and a dash of mythology, no matter if she's writing about Celtic gods, cat shifters, or the streets of Edinburgh.

When she's not typing away at her favourite cafe, Skye loves dried mango, as much exotic tea as she can squeeze into her cupboards, and being covered in pet hair by her demon cat Sootie.

Subscribe to her newsletter:
skyemackinnon.com/newsletter

Join her Facebook group:
facebook.com/groups/skyesbookharem

ABOUT LAURA GREENWOOD

Laura is a USA Today Bestselling Author of paranormal, fantasy, and urban fantasy romance (though she can occasionally be found writing contemporary romance). When she's not writing, she drinks a lot of tea, tries to resist French macarons, and works towards a diploma in Egyptology. She lives in the UK, where most of her books are set.

Follow the Author

- Website: www.authorlauragreenwood.co.uk
- Mailing List: www.authorlauragreenwood.co.uk/p/mailing-list-sign-up.html
- Facebook Group: http://facebook.com/groups/theparanormalcouncil

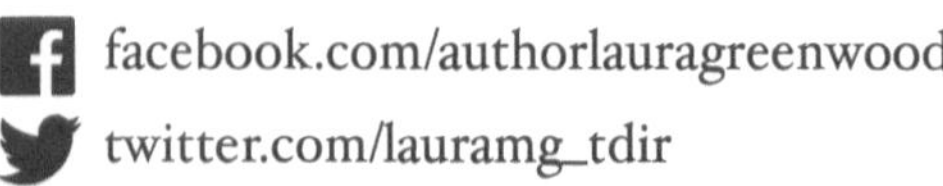 facebook.com/authorlauragreenwood

twitter.com/lauramg_tdir

instagram.com/authorlauragreenwood

bookbub.com/authors/laura-greenwood

amazon.com/author/lauragreenwood